Siân

Happy Reading

YES

Claire Highton-Stevenson

Claire ♡

www.itsclastevofficial.co.uk

ISBN: 9781724166609

DEDICATION

My Girl Gang
Live, Laugh, Love

My Aunty Jean, who sadly passed away Sept 2018.

ACKNOWLEDGMENTS

Michelle Arnold
May Dawney
Carol Hutchinson – Cam's biggest fan

Chapter One

"I don't care where, I am only concerned with when. So, when you have decided where you want us to get married, just let me know and I will be there," the blonde woman making coffee threw over her shoulder.

Camryn Thomas was being stubborn, and it was irritating Michelle Hamilton no end.

"Jesus Christ Camryn, this is your wedding too!" the irate brunette all but screamed, her sultry voice turning a little hoarser as her vocals reached a higher decibel. The actress was in no mood for her fiancée's indifference.

Taking a deep breath, Cam pivoted to face Michelle. She didn't want to continue this and end up with an argument when there were so many other, more important things that they could be doing, like taking their clothes off and going back to bed. She moved swiftly and closed the space to where the darker of the two sat at the island. Reaching out, she took her hand between her own and kissed her knuckles tenderly.

"Babe, I love you. I really, really love you, and I want nothing more than to be your wife and for you to wear my ring, but I just want to do it! Where we do it will make no difference to me because the only thing I will have my eyes on is you. Not the venue, not the scenery, and not the guests. Just you!"

"I fucking hate it when you do that," Michelle growled, her brown eyes fixed firmly upon her lover's as her arms flailed theatrically. It was a cloudy winter's day and her eyes did no more than complement it with the storm brewing in their depths.

"What? When I do what?" Cam asked, perplexed yet again. Sometimes she just had to admire the way that Michelle could quite easily flip into her over dramatic alter ego, Shelly Hamlin, a little too easily when she wanted her own way.

Camryn just wanted to get married. She had thought that was what Michelle wanted too, but since informing her mother, along with her agent and friend, Janice Rashbrook, the wedding had gotten a life of its own and now it was threatening to turn into the celebrity version of a royal wedding. It was something Cam really didn't want, but would go along with if it made her lover happy. She would do just about anything to make Michelle happy.

With them having met just a few months earlier, a lot of people might have thought they were rushing into it, but Cam didn't care what they thought. She knew what she wanted, and when she wanted something she would generally do all she could to get it. Being married to Michelle was no different.

Michelle had similar feelings; being a TV star had put enough limitations on her life already. Now she was finally in a place she wanted to be: loved and settled, and nobody was taking it away from her. It was still too fresh in her mind just how close she came to losing Camryn. The attack, by Cam's ex-girlfriend from back home in the UK, had left her half-dead, lying in a pool of her own blood, and it had left deep scars on both of them. In Camryn's case it was both figuratively and physically.

Jessica Montgomery had set about terrorising Michelle in an attempt to split them up and have Cam return to England with her. It failed of course. Unaware that Jessica was Michelle's stalker, Camryn had made it clear to her ex that she wasn't interested in her on several occasions, but she just wouldn't take the hint and then, just after Christmas, she had attacked Camryn.

The anger and venom with which Jessica attacked was shocking enough in itself, but to do it while Cam was in charge of entertaining Michelle's brother's kids had made things a whole lot worse. Being on the run, nobody had expected that she would try again, but she did. Now, she was safely locked away being assessed and Cam was finally able to think about the future.

"When you say something so fucking beautiful and yet still manage to be so fucking annoying." Michelle's face at this moment was stuck between wanting to smile and wanting to scream. She was just beautiful, and Cam couldn't help but smile as she leant in to kiss her soft, supple lips. Sucking the bottom one between her own when she pulled away, she left Michelle wanting more.

"You are beautiful, you're all I want and need. I will marry you anywhere you want to do it. If it makes you happy, it makes me happy."

"I hate you."

"You love me." Cam smiled and stepped in close. "You love me and you know it."

"I do love you," she agreed before Cam enthusiastically kissed her again. Tongues that knew the dance so well quickly found the rhythm they both enjoyed. "I know what you're doing," Michelle said, breaking the kiss, her arms locked firmly around Cam's neck.

"Hmm and what would that be?" Cam replied as her mouth moved from its original target to its next, Michelle's neck. She always did love her neck. The way it curved up from her shoulder into her hairline was just too enticing to ignore.

"You're trying to distract me with sex," the actress said, a slight whimper accompanying her words.

"Sex?" she inquired as her tongue licked a path downward from ear to collarbone, delighting in the small hollow she knew would be waiting for her. "Distract you from what?" Cam kissed her way across her pulse point, sucking gently before continuing up until she found a lonely ear lobe needing attention.

"Oh God, you know what that does to me?" Michelle shivered as goosebumps speckled her skin and her stomach clenched with arousal. Nobody had ever had this effect on her before.

"I do, it is true. I love how it affects you...how *I* affect you." She smiled against her skin. This was what she was born to do: to spend as long as possible teasing and tempting Michelle Hamilton.

"And distracts me."

"Distracts you?"

"Hmm hmm." Michelle hoped she would never get used to the effect Cam had on her; her body was just in tune with her. Cam's fingers, her mouth and her voice. She just had to look at her with those blue eyes, clear as crystal that would bore into her, and Michelle would feel an urging to just submit to anything her fiancée wanted of her. Yes, Camryn Thomas had a way about her that Michelle Hamilton couldn't get enough of.

"So, what was it you were telling me?" Cam asked, trying to concentrate and give her undivided attention to her fiancée. She extricated herself and went back to the task she had started earlier: making coffee for them both, leaving Michelle aroused but grateful to be back on track with the wedding plans.

"I was *asking* you what your opinion of the Padua Hills theatre was for the wedding." She passed a brochure over to Cam, who placed it down on the table, and tried desperately not to imagine Camryn pulling her clothes off. "Please don't make instant, it really is horrible when you do it." Cam glared for a second before grinning. Apparently, her coffee-making skills where lacking.

"Okay, firstly are you asking me because it is somewhere you really like, or because Janice and your mother like it?" she asked, turning her attention to the machine that made perfectly flawless coffee.

"Well, I admit it was Janice that suggested it. However, I think it's quite nice."

"Quite nice? Not amazing or fantastic, just quite nice? Are you happy enough with quite nice?" she teased gently. "Though to be fair, you did call our first kiss 'nice,' so I'm not sure how to take it when you say 'quite nice?'" She laughed before she continued, dodging a playful spank to her butt. "Seriously babe, I just want you to have the best, not 'quite nice.' I want to see your face light up when you show me something because when that happens, I will be ecstatic. So, can we agree to chill out a bit, take our time and find the place that's 'us?'"

"But Camryn, what you fail to understand is that a lot of these places are all booked years in advance, and it will be hard to find somewhere at such short notice!" Michelle whined, actually whined like a child, but the grin that went with it suggested she knew what she was doing.

"Ok listen, I want to marry you as soon as possible, but I am willing to hold off if it means you getting your dream wedding."

"Will you please just look at the brochures though, I want your input. We could pick three and then go and visit them and see when the earliest is we can book."

"Ok."

"Ok?"

"Yes, on one condition," Cam said in all seriousness, her head nodding slowly as a sly grin developed on her lips.

Narrowing her eyes suspiciously, Michelle asked the question. "And what would that be exactly?"

"Well." She waggled her eyebrows.

Michelle took a moment. She knew exactly what Cam was wanting from her. With a smirk she grabbed the hem of her top and lifted it up and over her head. "You have got 15 minutes and then we are going to look through these brochures, got it?"

"Yes, my love," she answered, unhooking the red satin bra that stood between her and her prize. "I fucking love your boobs," she said as she bent slightly to take a hardened nipple between her lips.

"You are so rude." Michelle gasped; she loved this feeling. She hadn't always enjoyed the attention a lover lavished on her breasts, but Cam was different, tender in her movements. No less aggressive or passionate when required, but always tender.

"What is it with the name-calling? I am hurt." Cam feigned sadness, her bottom lip jutting out and quivering before turning into a giant smile. "Now if you could be a love and remove the rest of your clothing, I would be a very happy girlfriend."

Michelle took her time to extricate herself from her tight-fit jeans and underwear. She slowed her movements, enjoying the slight fidget Cam had going on as she took a step back to relish the show.

With her arousal being fuelled to the extreme by this mini strip, Cam wasted no time in grabbing hold of Michelle by the waist and pressing her up against the kitchen counter. She took hold of her buttocks as she moved in for a kiss. A kiss so thorough that Michelle barely noticed she was being hoisted up onto the worktop. The marble was cold against her bare skin, and she gasped out loud as Cam slid her to the edge of the counter. Camryn broke the kiss, the need for air and to move lower encompassing all of her thoughts. Her mouth found its goal in an instant.

"Oh Jesus, Cam, so good." Michelle's voice was low and smoky as she relaxed into the sensations coursing through her right now. She had no control over her hips as they moved by their own will to create the perfect rhythm that would take her where she wanted to go.

This was one of Cam's favourite things to do: tasting her lover, hearing the way she moaned and how she writhed as her hands flew to Cam's hair and held her in place. Cam was more turned on than she had ever been before, with anyone!

"Baby, you're going to make me come," Michelle gasped as Cam's tongue swept around her heated core, teasing and nudging her toward a pleasure she was well aware she wanted.

"That's the plan," Cam boasted, as she swapped her tongue for fingers, rocking into her when their lips crashed together in a searing kiss once more.

"So...close...baby please...Oh God, Camryn please." Cam heard her pleas and doubled her efforts. Her bicep burned, but she refused to give in. Her training had been building her muscle strength up, and she was determined to get back to where they were before Jessica tried to ruin everything.

"Fuck yes!! Right there, baby!" Michelle cried out. She shuddered and collapsed forwards, her hands wrapped tightly around Cam. She loved to climax like that, knowing that Cam knew her so well and cared enough to want her to climax like that.

None of her other lovers had ever spent so much time and effort trying to understand what got her off, but Camryn did. Cam would try anything and everything to make sure Michelle was spent, sated. She would gorge on her; her body would be left drained and exhausted and she would wake feeling more content that she had ever done.

Cam took Michelle's face in her hands and kissed her gently. She let her hands wander down Michelle's torso and under her thighs. Wrapping them around her own waist, she lifted her and carried her to the couch. She lowered Michelle to lie down, then climbed on the couch with her and pulled their bodies close together.

"Damn you, Camryn!" Michelle muttered, twisting herself around to burrow into her lover's side.

"What have I done now? Ya know most people's girlfriends would be grateful for the orgasm you just had!"

"Oh, you can trust me, lover, I am very grateful and very, *very*, satisfied. However, I now just want to sleep, snuggled with you here for a while when we *should* be looking through brochures."

"Ah I see, how cruel of me?" She smiled and made a grab for the blanket that lay along the back of the couch. She tucked the blanket around them both and thought about how just a few days ago they were so far apart emotionally and physically. They both worried Cam would never come out of the funk she had found herself in with regard to how her body now looked. "I like this, just us," she whispered, then added "What about Vegas?"

"Camryn Thomas!" Michelle said without opening her eyes. "I had better be dreaming that you just suggested Las Vegas as a destination for our wedding!"

Camryn kissed her cheek, smiling, and said nothing more. Everything was just how it should be.

Chapter Two

Since winning her millions on the Euro Lotto two years earlier, Cam had enjoyed a lifestyle that for many was out of the question, but she had never abused it. She had never taken too much advantage of the power that came with wealth. Until now, because now she had something far more important than money to protect. She had Michelle, and she had already come close to losing her twice now. Once when Jessica attacked, and she had almost died herself, and then again in the aftermath when she hadn't been able to deal with it and had pushed Michelle away.

"Camryn? Are you okay?" Michelle asked, concerned, the light knock on the door making her jump.

"Yes, I'm fine, just coming," she said, quickly brushing her teeth before she finally unlocked the door. Passing Michelle, she jumped into bed and pulled the covers up to her chin. She closed her eyes and tried desperately not to see the hurt on Michelle's face. She failed.

As she jumped into bed and hid beneath the covers, she knew that Michelle was crying alone in the bathroom, and all because she had no idea how to get past the disgust she had for herself whenever she looked in the mirror.

They had weathered that storm. The fallout from finding herself at death's door had been a bout of reactions that had threatened to tear Camryn apart. Depression and an unfathomable shame had caused a giant gulf between them until the actress had had enough and forced the issue.

"I want to tell you something I was thinking about last night," she said to Cam, "Do you remember this?" she said, pointing to her knee, "and this," she said again, pointing to her naked shoulder. "Do you remember what you told me about them? That you loved me, every part of me?" She waited for Cam

to acknowledge her words, to start to see where this was going. "Why do you think that would be any different for me with you?"

"Because you are perfect," Cam said simply without even having to think.

"Camryn, Baby." She reached out for her hand. "I am far from perfect, but I believe you think I am, just as I love every part of you equally as much."

The blonde considered her words before she spoke next. "I don't want you to pity me, I don't want to see pity in your eyes when you look at me."

"I do not pity you, I love you." Cam's gaze moved away, and so she brought it back again. Her palms caressed each cheek and guided her eyes back so she could fix on them. "I watched in the park as paramedics worked to keep you alive. I sat by your bed not knowing if you would wake up. If you have scars to prove that you're alive and here with me then I will worship every single one of them, because losing you in any way, shape, or form is just not conceivable to me." Michelle's words hit home.

Now, they were back on track and Camryn was feeling stronger both in body and mind. Jessica was now locked up. But still, Cam felt it was down to her to make sure that Michelle would never have to face what she had had to.

Stabbed eight times in the chest, one of the wounds had pierced her lung and in turn had caused her heart to stop, twice. Thankfully it wasn't her turn to die that day, and through whatever miracle it was, she made a full recovery. But it had forced a lot of changes to her life, changes she had never considered necessary before.

The basement area of their home had been nothing more than a storage space and wine cellar before the attack. It now housed gym equipment and a sauna. It never ceased to amaze

Camryn just how quickly you could have something done when you had the money to pay for it. Her fitness levels were gradually getting better, her strength returning, and she was back to light training. There were still limitations on what she could and couldn't do, but it was better, and most of that was down to Michelle and the strict regime she kept her on.

What she wasn't happy about were the constant people around her. She knew right now that it was necessary, but she didn't like it. The only reason she didn't complain too much was because of the man in charge of them all. A man she would trust with her life.

"Hey, can you spot me?" Cam asked the tall blonde guy that stood next to the weights she wanted to use. Her trainer was pushing her to lift heavier, and she wanted to get a session in.

"Yeah, sure. What weight?" he asked, moving to help load up the other side of the bar to the one she was working.

"20 either side." She watched as he loaded up the correct weights. "Camryn," she added. He looked a little confused.

"Huh?"

"My name, it's Camryn. Or Cam, whatever." She grinned and took up position on the bench, reaching for the barbell, ready to begin her lift.

"Oh, right. Gavin, Gavin Grogan."

He had been in the army, a career soldier until an incident left him considering his options, but civilian life wasn't that great either and, unable to get a full-time job, he was pretty much sleeping in his car. Cam gave him a job working the door at OUT. She set him up in an apartment and from then on, they had held a deep respect for each other. He was honourable and loyal and the closest she would ever get to having a brother. All the qualities in a person that Camryn now looked for in people, she found in Gavin.

She prided herself now on the people she had in her life. People that had helped bring her out of a life without trust and love. Her life had turned full circle from the life she had left behind in London just a few years prior. She shuddered as she remembered that fateful day that had put into action a sequence of events she could never have envisaged.

The room was in darkness, almost. The curtains were still drawn with just the bedside lamp to illuminate the events in front of her as she witnessed the definitive betrayal. On top of the pink and white duvet – the one they had bought together in the first week they moved here – on her fucking bed lay her girlfriend. She was naked, legs spread wide with her best friend knelt neatly between them, her torso bent low, long black hair tossed to one side. It was pretty clear what she was doing. There would be no need for the lesbian sex manual in order to work it out.

But in hindsight, their betrayal had been the best thing to ever happen to Camryn Thomas. She got rich, she moved to LA, and she fell in love with a movie star. It was the stuff of dreams. She smiled as she thought of Michelle again. Her face seemed to ache these days with the constant happiness she felt, until Jessica had forced her way back into their lives.

Jessica had been fixated on Michelle. Stalking her, sending malicious photographs and letters. And yet, it had been Camryn that she had attacked.

Elevated to the position of security manager, Gavin was now in charge of a team of twelve. Twelve highly trained personal bodyguards. It was his job to maintain security at the club and wherever Michelle or Camryn went. She hated it of course, and would end it soon enough. But, there was no amount of money that she wouldn't spend, if it meant keeping Michelle safe.

Chapter Three

Tuesday morning found Cam sleeping late. Startled from her slumber by the constant chiming of something annoying in the background of her dream, she forced her eyes to open. Staring straight at the clock, its big red numbers read: *late.*

"Shit!" she yelled, her eyes wide as saucers as she jumped out of bed and ran, naked, to the bathroom. She skidded to a halt before turning back around to run right back into the bedroom and pick up the annoying dinging.

"Hello!" she said sheepishly. Big trouble - that's what she was in. Absolutely huge, immense trouble.

"Camryn, where are you?" Michelle asked. She sounded worried and for a moment, Cam was hopeful.

"I...uh I...I just woke up," she finally admitted, rubbing at her eyes she blinked the last remnants of sleep away.

"Oh for the love of God Cam, you were supposed to be here 15 minutes ago. I was worried sick!"

"I know. I'm so sorry, the alarm went off and I thought I hit snooze, but I must have turned it off instead. I can be there in 30 minutes."

"Fine, I'll see if we can rearrange to view in 30 minutes, but I am warning you Camryn, if you're late I am withdrawing my body and therefore sex for a week, do you understand me?" Michelle hissed a whispered ultimatum down the line.

"Yes, fully understood. The implications of my arriving any later are unsurmountable and I am on my way right now." She hung up the phone, slightly perturbed at just how turned on she was from that little exchange.

She jumped into the shower, and having barely gotten wet she was dried and dressed, ready to head out the door. She had 22 minutes left to get to The Wayfarers Chapel or life wouldn't be worth living.

"Late again, Camryn?" her housekeeper and mother figure Maria called after her as the blonde rushed past in a blur of lateness and leather.

The diminutive woman that stood at the door was looking at her as though there was something very wrong. Cam had been interviewing potential housekeepers all morning and quite frankly, she could do without the look of irritation the woman was giving her. Her CV was impeccable though, and Cam was loath to turn her away based solely on her tired annoyance.

"Did you iron that?" the woman, Maria Flores, asked her. Cam looked down at her shirt and the creases that said she hadn't.

"Uh, no I uh..."

"Take it off," she said, standing and placing her bag down onto the couch. "I do it, you can't interview people looking like you fell out of bed."

Cam was astounded and yet, she found herself unbuttoning the shirt and handing it over to her.

"Where you keep the iron?" Cam led her to the small utility room where all her cleaning materials were stored and watched in awe as the woman got the board out and the shirt ironed in mere minutes. "This room is a mess. I tell you what? I clean...you like, then I get the job."

During her time in LA, there weren't many people that told Cam what she would or wouldn't do. Sometimes, she missed it, having someone looking out for her.

"Okay, deal."

"You know me! Catch ya later, Maria." The petite woman grinned back and shook her head slowly as she watched her employer run out of the house.

There was only one way that Camryn was going to salvage the possibility of her sex life continuing, and that was to take the bike. The Yamaha roared into life the second the ignition was engaged. She shoved the helmet on over her head and without another pause, Cam was on her way.

It was actually a beautiful day for riding a motorbike. The sun was shining bright and high in the sky, it was warm, and the streets in LA were made for weaving in and out of traffic. She accelerated and felt the breeze against her face. Her visor was open just enough to create instant air con and avoid any flying insects from smashing into her face.

She accomplished her mission with 3 minutes to spare. Now, she just had to find them. It was a tight timescale, but she managed it. She found them in a small clearing in the woods, sitting together at a picnic table, huddled in a conspiracy of gossip. Janice cackled and tossed her head back as Martha finished speaking and joined her in a guffaw that was loud enough to cause heads to turn.

Janice was the first to notice her. The short woman stood from her seat and gave her a sound hug. Michelle glared at her from where she sat, but released a deep breath of relief as she finally set eyes on her blond goddess. She watched as her own mother stood next to greet the woman that would soon become her second daughter-in-law.

"Cutting it fine, Camryn," Michelle said, before she too finally stood, smiling at last. She kissed her, breathing her in and melting into the safety of her arms.

"I'm sorry," Cam whispered in her ear as they embraced.

"It's okay, I'm not mad at you," she replied, "Anymore!" Her eyebrow raised into a perfect arch. "But, had I had to endure a week without sex..."

"Damn, it's sexy when you get all bossy like that." Her playful wink didn't go down as well as she had hoped when Michelle glared some more. Camryn understood that she was pushing her luck right about now.

"Good morning," boomed a deep voice from behind her. A man stood there in a well-tailored suit, with a clipboard and an air of authority surrounding him. "I'm Michael Shale and I am the duty manager here at Wayfarers. I understand that you would like to check out the facilities and see if we fit the requirements you need for your upcoming nuptials?"

"Yes, that would be perfect," Michelle answered. "We've had a look around earlier at the grounds, so it would be great if you could show us the rest of the facilities."

Michael took great pride in taking them around the grounds and pointing out places of interest. The chapel itself was beautiful, surrounded by a wooden frame housing giant glass windows to allow the guest to feel 'at one' with nature. It truly was beautiful.

"So, what did you think?" Cam asked Michelle as they walked towards the car park, arm-in-arm.

"It's beautiful and I could see us getting married there, but..."

"But?"

"But, I don't know that I want to have two venues. They can't hold the reception here, and it would mean asking everyone to find their way to a separate venue. I think I would prefer it all to be held in one place."

"I agree," Janice butted in. "The media will be all over this too, you two are not now just the latest news because of who Michelle is; this whole thing with you almost being killed by your crazy ex has meant that the media is now interested in you also, so the less opportunity you give the press to invade your privacy, the better."

Cam had always known Janice was a no-nonsense, say-it-how-it-is kind of woman, and she applauded her for it usually, but on this occasion, it caused her to flinch hearing her speak of Jessica so freely. She found herself searching out Michelle's hand and gripping it tightly. Michelle rubbed her thumb over the back of Cam's hand soothingly and took a step closer to her, letting her know she was there and that she was aware.

Martha had noticed the subtle change in Cam too, and the look of concern on her daughter's face only made to prove the point. "I agree, and I think maybe it is wise for us all to get moving to the next venue. We don't want to be late again, do we?" she said with a smile, trying to instil a little light-hearted humour to hopefully nudge the fear from Camryn's mind.

"Do you want to leave the bike here, darling, and come with us in the car?" Michelle asked gently.

It took Cam a few seconds to register that someone was talking to her. Finally, she looked to Michelle and smiled. "No, I...I'm fine, really. I will meet you there." She was ok, that was something she had to remind herself now and then. "I'm okay, I promise."

"Okay, if you're sure?" Michelle looked her right in the eye and held her gaze.

"I promise," Cam assured her. She swung a leg over her bike and got comfortable as she waited for the others to make their way to the car.

"You'll follow us in the car?" Michelle enquired.

"Sure." She gave Michelle a quick grin before pulling on her helmet.

"Okay, I love you."

"I love you too."

She sat there on the bike waiting. Much to Cam's amusement, the three women got into the car, and after a minute of reapplying lipsticks and checking hair, they finally proceeded to drive out of the carpark with Cam following closely behind.

They headed back towards Santa Monica and Hangar 8, an old airfield that now used its space for functions and just about anything you wanted to hire it for. It was basically a blank canvas.

After wandering around and being shown a short film by the owner and manager detailing some of the previous events and what they had been able to turn Hangar 8 in to, they sat down for a coffee.

"I like it," Cam said. "It's like a film set that hasn't had the scene laid out yet."

"I like it too; do you have any ideas of what we could do here?" Michelle asked. She spun around like a ballerina as she tried to take it all in. Cam smiled at her antics; she loved to see Michelle excited, and that thought was what turned her smile into a frown. "What? What is it?" Michelle asked, noting the change in Cam's demeanour.

"It's nothing, I just...It's all so sterile, and that means we will have to really work at turning this into something that represents us and makes this the fairy-tale venue."

"Yeah, but we can get that done."

"And how long will that take? The earliest we can get this is June and even then, it's a date we don't get a say in because it's a date someone else cancelled their wedding, doesn't that seem like bad luck to you?" Michelle listened intently as Cam explained her feelings. Deflated, she looked around once more.

"I guess, but Cam, all of these venues are going to be difficult to get at short notice and anyway, we still need time to plan and organise everything. Four months is really not that long at all."

"It is, it's a lifetime." She reached for the brunette's hands, holding them gently as she continued. "I want to marry you now, not in June. I don't want to wait till next week, I'd do it right now if we could." Michelle melted a little at the woman that stood in front of her pleading her case.

"You are so adorable. I love you Camryn, I want the same thing, I do, but it just isn't possible sweetheart." Cam considered that. The very concept of impossible meant little to her nowadays. Impossible was a word that meant challenging. She could make things happen if she paid enough, worked hard enough, and asked the right people.

"Do you trust me?"

Michelle tilted her head and pursed her lips. "You know I do."

"And if you could marry me next week, would you?" Cam continued, a plan forming in her mind.

"Yes, but—" She felt a finger touch her lips. Cam stood in front of her smiling like an idiot.

"No buts, let's get married next Friday."

"Camryn, I am not running off to Vegas! Nor am I doing it without our friends and family there. Can you not just be a little patient?"

"Nope, I want to go to bed every night with my wife." Martha and Janice watched from the side lines as both women went back and forth in discussion. Whatever Cam had just said to her daughter made Martha smile as she watched the reaction on Michelle's lips. The biggest beam appeared, and she moved in close, wrapping her arms around Cam's neck. It was still a little strange observing her baby girl in the arms of another woman, but she reminded herself each time that she had never seen her child look so happy and therefore, she didn't care which gender her daughter had fallen in love with.

"So, you want to get married on Friday... what about my dress? I will never get a dress made in time."

"Leave everything to me. I promise you, you will get married somewhere romantic. Somewhere that's unique to us *and* with all our friends and family there."

Chapter Four

Camryn woke early the following day. Michelle lay sleeping on her side, her face relaxed and at peace. When they had returned home the previous afternoon, there had been a buzz of excitement as Cam filled Maria in on all the decisions they had made.

They had bounced ideas off one another until Cam had a firm awareness of what she needed to accomplish in the next few days. It wasn't going to be easy at all, but it was doable.

She climbed out of bed, grabbing the phone as she left the room, not wanting to disturb Michelle. It was daylight, and that meant it was time to start the process of wedding planning. She could feel a bubble of excitement building as she flicked the phone screen into life and dialled the first number.

"Morning Janice, it's Camryn Thomas, I wanted to ask a favour." She spoke confidently into the phone, holding it in the crook of her neck as she grabbed a pen and some paper. Her coffee cup sat steaming on the countertop next to where she sat, along with an apple that she rolled back and forth with one finger.

"Oh really? And what would that be?" The jovial reply made Cam smile and she picked up the apple and tossed it into the air, catching it, before repeating the action.

"Well, I am sure you're aware that I'm head over heels in love with Michelle."

"I am aware of that, yes," Janice replied with a smile. "As much as it may surprise you, I do have a love life too, so I am very aware of how happy you are."

"Really? Well that is something I am very happy to hear more about sometime." Cam placed the apple back on the countertop and poured some cereal in a bowl. She added milk and was reminded of home: cornflakes and cold milk for breakfast in the kitchen by herself. Caroline was away at Uni, her father already out of the house and at work, her mother catching up on her sleep.

"Uh huh, I am sure. So, what can I do for you?"

"Okay, so, I had an idea about the wedding and I need you to help me organise it."

"I'm listening."

~Yes~

That afternoon, Michelle was whisked off to the fanciest bridal shop in town. She was measured from top to toe, and then she was seated on a comfortable couch with a glass of champagne and a platter of canapes. Beside her sat her mother, Janice, Jen, and her friend, Lisa Marconi.

The ladies sat back and enjoyed an exceptionally entertaining fashion show. Model after model paraded through the lounge in every wedding dress they had to offer, until Michelle decided upon the dress she wanted. Between them they had agreed that they didn't need to have bridesmaids or anyone else involved in the wedding. They didn't want to be walked down an aisle or have an entourage of bridesmaids; all they needed was each other, and their guests to act as witness.

When Cam had first suggested her plan, Michelle was nervous. She trusted Cam and she knew that she would put everything she had into getting it done, and getting done right, but that didn't mean she wasn't worried about the potential for it to be too much too soon. Now though, as the champagne flowed and the dresses were paraded in front of her, she felt a new-found confidence that if anyone could pull this off, Cam could and would.

Over the following couple of days, whenever she broached the subject with her lover about how things were going, she would receive a big grin and a kiss to her cheek, and a few words along the lines of, "It's all under control." And so, she went with it, trusting that whatever Camryn came up with, she would love anyway.

By Thursday night she was bursting with excitement. Cam had been out all day long finalising everything that needed doing. It was all still a huge secret. Even Maria was banned from speaking about anything she might have seen or overheard, and with her brandishing her towel anytime Michelle dared to try and prise anything from her, it quickly became apparent that the housekeeper wouldn't be giving away any insider information to her anytime soon.

When the door finally swung open, Camryn almost staggered inside and slumped down on the couch beside her. She checked her watch. 9 p.m.

"Hey." She smiled tiredly.

"Hey, yaself." Michelle grinned back. "You look tired. Maybe we should have an early night?"

"I'd love one, but...we have somewhere else to be right now."

"Really? Intriguing...lead on then." Michelle smirked. Standing, she held out a hand for Cam to take and pulled her lover to her feet. Face to face, she took the opportunity to kiss her. Soft lips pressed eagerly and the kiss deepened easily. Forcing some self-control into her tired being, Cam pulled away and smiled, taking hold of Michelle's hand to lead her back out of the house to the waiting car.

"So, tradition dictates that couples should spend the night before their wedding apart," Cam explained as Gavin drove them steadily along through the evening traffic. The giant wheel of Santa Monica Pier loomed up into the darkening night sky as they cruised slowly along. She watched the look of disappointment wash over her soon-to-be wife's face and giggled. "But, I don't ever want to spend a night out of your arms ever again, so...I figured we would just spend our last night as singles, together and away from everyone else."

"Good, because you may well be tired and not able to do any more than sleep tonight, but I *really* want to be in your arms when you do," Michelle admitted.

The brunette smiled to herself as Gavin pulled up alongside the yacht. It was perfect. Their first night spent together on-board had been the catalyst to where they were today.

They climbed out of the car, and with arms wrapped around one another, they strolled up the gangplank. At the very top stood Captain Henderson.

"Welcome aboard." He smiled and tipped his hat. "Everything is as you wished, Ms Thomas."

"John, ya know you can call me Camryn?" She held out her hand to shake his.

"I know and yet, Ms Thomas just seems to flow from me." He grinned and wrapped his other palm around their joined hands, giving her a conspiratorial wink before stepping aside and waving them on.

The deck was alight with fairy lights that danced and bobbed as the boat moved gracefully with the gentle tides ebbing and flowing. It looked magical, but Michelle barely had time to notice before she was whisked inside and down the stairs that lead to the master suite.

Laughing like children, the pair of them almost fell through the small door as Cam grabbed her around the waist and swung her around. Pulling her tightly against her own body, she held tight. "You look beautiful right now," Cam whispered against her lips, pressing gently to seal the kiss.

"I feel beautiful whenever I am with you," she answered, adding another kiss before Cam spoke again. Her arms snaked up and around Cam's neck as she enjoyed the embrace.

"Good, because..." Cam smiled and held her gaze. Michelle's head tilted as she considered what Cam might be about to say next. "I need you to get showered and changed."

"Oh, have we got a dirty little plan for the night ahead?" she teased as her mouth ghosted from Cam's ear down her jawline, sending shivers down her spine.

"Jesus, yes..." she mumbled as their mouths came together once more. The kiss was deep, and intent was made instantly as Michelle's fingers moved to the hem of Cam's shirt and began to tug. "But..." Cam said, breaking the kiss and stilling her hands. "First, we need to get married."

The engines fired up and the boat began to move slowly away from the harbour wall that it had been held firmly against minutes earlier.

"First thing we're going to do tomorrow, right?" Michelle asked, leaning back in for a further kiss. But Cam held firm, placing her palm against her lover's chest and pressing firmly to stop her advances.

"Actually, in about 3 hours."

"What?"

"Midnight, the moment it turns Friday..."

"Hold on, I don't understand...how? What about our friends, my parents?" Michelle, seeming a little dazed, let herself fall into a seated position on the bed.

"Well, it's pretty simple really..." Cam began as she took a seat next to her. "We are currently heading out to meet everybody else, they're waiting for us on another boat. Along with officiates and a band. Once we draw up alongside then everyone will come aboard, and we will exchange our vows."

"But..." Cam placed a finger gently against her lips to still them.

Smiling, she continued. "And then they will leave for the night and return tomorrow, where we will spend the day at sea partying until the sun sets again."

"You're serious, aren't you?" Michelle said. Her face looked concerned, and for a moment Camryn worried that she had gotten this all wrong.

"Deadly," she countered, breath held as she waited for Michelle to consider this plan. It seemed to take an age as every option and scenario ran through her head. "What about my make-up? Hair? My dress? I mean I need help, I can't just take a shower and throw anything on." She was rambling, but she wasn't saying no, and now Cam smiled and let out the long-held breath.

"Michelle, take a breath, babe." She laughed as she took hold of her hands and brought them to her lips; she kissed them both. "I have it all under control." She rapped her knuckles on the door and in an instant, it opened. Three women entered carrying bags and cases. "This is Carla, Marie, and Valezra. Hair, make-up, and stylist. Your dress is hanging in the wardrobe. Everything you need is here... now I need to leave you to it so that I too can make myself look pretty."

"Wait," she said before Cam could leave. "Can you give us a minute?" she asked the ladies. They backed out quietly, leaving the two women alone once more. "You are the most amazing person I have ever known. I will marry you at midnight. I would marry you wearing a trash bag and baseball cap if it meant that in less than three hours I will be Mrs Thomas. Because that's what I want Cam, yours in every way."

The kiss that followed left them both wanting more and wishing the rest of the night away. "That's a reminder...of what's coming later." Michelle smirked and bit her bottom lip as she opened the door and pushed Camryn out.

Chapter Five

As the yacht drew up alongside the larger boat already anchored and waiting, Cam stood beside Captain Henderson to welcome them their guests aboard.

Between Michelle's parents and Janice, Cam had been able to invite every single person on Michelle's list. It was all pretty simple in the end. They spent an afternoon phoning around until they had a yes or no answer from every single invite.

Standing there in the almost-darkness, Cam looked around her. The boat was perfect and everything Cam had envisioned it to be. Gavin and the rest of the team had worked their butts off to make sure that every fairy light twinkled. The entire deck was covered in bright little lights that glowed brighter against the night sky. As the water ebbed beneath them and the boat rose and fell gently, they looked like tiny fireflies. It was beautiful.

She caught a glimpse of herself in the window and sucked in a breath. Her palms brushed down her chest and she fingered her lapels. The black fitted suit she wore was impeccable. She had taken a lot of inspiration from their first public appearance. It was a look she could pull off any day of the week. Right now though, she felt a little suffocated by it. Expelling a deep breath, Erin turned to her.

"You okay?"

"Yeah." She nodded, biting her bottom lip. "Just nervous I guess."

"What the hell for? You're marrying the love of your life, who I might add is hot as hell and totally into you. This is a breeze, my friend." She slapped Cam on the back and laughed. "In a few minutes you're going to look up and see her and she's gonna take your breath away. That's when ya can get nervous, if ya can't breathe! Otherwise, Cam? Just enjoy it. She said yes."

"You're right, she said yes," Cam agreed and then mumbled to herself, "Always, yes."

First across the gangplank were the staff for the evening, waiting staff and the musicians. Their instruments were already aboard and set up. They would play gentle classical music as guests filed across and they waited for the ceremony to begin. Then they would continue through the service, accompanying the ceremony with a beautiful rendition of "Pachelbel's Canon" in D major. It was one of Cam's favourite pieces.

Finally, the guests began to make their way across the gangplank.

Martha and Bob came first with Maria not far behind them. Martha clung to Bob like her life depended on it. The wooden bridge between the two boats was very sturdy, but she wasn't so sure, and so she clung to her husband's arm.

"Camryn, you look perfect." Maria took her face within her palms. "You both are going to have such a wonderful life together. She fits you."

"I know, thank you for making me..."

Maria swatted at her and tutted. "You just needed a little push. I'll see you after." She winked and kissed her cheek before moving on to take a glass of champagne from a waiting tray.

The pianist began to play. "Yiruma's River Flows in You" echoed out into the night and Cam felt herself finally relax. A waitress appeared and offered her a glass of champagne. She took it and smiled. She was getting married, to Michelle. She had been so busy making it happen that it hadn't really sunk in until just now as the beautiful music washed over. Erin nudged her and grinned.

"Welcome aboard. Bride or bride?" she asked, laughing as the staff from OUT joined them. Janice and her date followed. Cam couldn't help but smirk at the sight of the usually put-together woman fussing over her date's tie, adjusting it for him. At one point, Cam seriously thought she was going to lick her thumb and wipe something from his face, she was so intent on making sure he looked decent.

"Janice and..."

"Christopher, this is Camryn Thomas," Michelle's agent stated quickly before Cam could make a joke at her expense.

Christopher shot out a hand and firmly grasped Cam's. "Nice to finally meet you, Jan here talks a lot about you both. I feel like I almost..."

"Well, maybe we should move along and let people get on board. Otherwise this wedding is never going to happen, and I don't have the time to go through this again. You owe me!" Janice grinned at Cam and tugged on Christopher's arm. Cam chuckled to herself as she watched him being dragged along the deck towards the bar.

"He seems nice," Erin giggled.

"Yeah, let's get him drunk later and find out more about Janice the girlfriend." Cam laughed. "You know there is more to her than that tough exterior, right?"

"Oh yeah, I bet she's a pussycat underneath it all." They fell about laughing, but Cam soon sobered as she looked up to see the next guests coming across the walkway, guests that Cam had been anxiously waiting for. When she had been injured, Michelle's niece and nephew were both with her. She hadn't seen either of them face to face since she had come out of hospital, and she couldn't wait. Dylan was being carried in her father's arms, and she waved shyly as they got closer to Cam. Her blonde hair was curled into little ringlets, and she was barely keeping her eyes open. Cam felt bad for not thinking this through more with regard to the kids. But, Robbie had assured her that it was fine. The kids would be okay for one night staying up late. They had made sure that both of them had had a nap earlier in the day, and the ceremony would only be for a few minutes, so it wasn't like they would be up all night.

She looked for Zac. She knew the whole thing had affected him more; he was older and had seen a lot more than they had first realised.

"Cam!!" he shouted as she came into view. He ran toward her, but came to a halt just shy of her. A worried look came across his face as he studied her.

"Hey, come here you." She dropped down to her knee and held her arms open, ready to grab a hold of him and hug him hard. But he held back from her still. "Hey Buddy, it's okay, I am all good now, see?" she said, holding her arms out wide. "You won't hurt me, I promise." He studied her for a second more, and with that promise he threw his arms around her neck. "I missed you," she said as her arms wrapped around his small frame.

"Missed you too. You really okay now?" he asked as he stared into her eyes. He looked so smart in his tiny suit, hair slicked back like his dad's. They had chatted several times over Skype, but it was the first time they could really lay eyes on one another.

"I am, I am really good, I promise." She smiled at him before eventually standing and greeting Jen and Rob.

"So, ready to marry my sister?" he asked with a grin that was just like Michelle's.

"You bet."

~Yes~

At exactly five minutes to midnight on the first Friday in March, Michelle appeared in her dress. She walked the short carpet that lead from the cabins to the stern of the boat and to Camryn. Her mass of raven curls was piled high on top of her head with flowers intertwined. She went without a veil. Her dress was simple: an off-white, off-the-shoulder sheath-style dress that dropped to the floor, accentuating every inch of her perfectly. Her father met her halfway. The proudest man alive at that moment.

"Daddy?"

"Pumpkin, you look beautiful," he said, using her childhood nickname. "You ready?"

"Yes," she said, with the certainty of someone who knew only good could come from this. She nodded before adding, "I have never been more ready in my life."

"She's a lucky woman, and I know that you didn't plan on having anyone walk you down an aisle, but would you make an old man happy and let him do it anyway?" he asked, a tear bulging and ready to fall any minute.

She blinked a few times, determined not to cry and ruin her make-up. She nodded, smiling as she leant forward and kissed her father's cheek. "The honour would be all mine."

Bob Hamilton held out his arm, and as his daughter took it, he reached across and patted her hand. "Just you wait till you see her."

"Really?"

"Oh yeah."

When Cam caught sight of her, she almost stopped breathing, and that was problematic if she was going to make it through the ceremony and marry this stunning apparition in front of her.

"You okay?" Erin asked as she leaned into her friend.

"Yeah, look at her," she replied in awe as she watched Bob lead her toward them. "Pinch me."

"What?" Erin questioned.

"Pinch me," Cam insisted, and then she flinched when she felt the small tweak on her arm. "Ow."

"Oh, don't be a baby."

Cam laughed before turning back to watch as Michelle moved effortlessly in her bare feet towards her.

Time stopped, the air stilled, and every step seemed to take an eon before finally Michelle was standing beside her and the officiate was speaking. Vows were offered and rings were exchanged along with smiles and a few tears. Beneath the light of the moon and the stars, two became one on this boat, and life as Mrs & Mrs Thomas began.

Chapter Six

It felt a little bit odd as the guests filed back across the gangplank to the waiting boat. The musicians played Chopin as everyone kissed and congratulated them. The newlyweds held hands and waved goodbye for now. In the morning they would meet again and have a fabulous champagne breakfast, before most of them congregated back on the yacht and spent the day at sea. Cam had booked a DJ and caterers. It was going to be epic, she was sure of it, something they would talk about for years to come.

Alone on the deck, Cam wrapped her arms around her new wife and, resting her chin upon her shoulder, she couldn't help the smile that lit up her face.

"Wanna go to bed, Mrs Thomas?" she whispered against the shell of her ear.

"God, yes." Michelle grinned, turning in her arms. "Let's go."

While the service had taken place, the bedroom had been tidied of all make-up and hair products. The bed was made and champagne had been left on ice. Cam popped the cork and poured them both a glass. When Michelle took one from her, she held hers up. "A toast. To us and to many more nights beneath the stars."

Michelle returned the smile Cam had given her and held up her own glass. "To us." She sipped hers, while Cam downed the lot. "Woah lady, no getting drunk on our wedding night. I have plans for you." She turned and faced the mirror, taking off her earrings as she watched Camryn.

Cam placed her palms gently upon Michelle's bare shoulders, squeezing gently as she contemplated her next move. "I've spent weeks imagining this very moment. There's no way I am missing it by being drunk. Drunk on love, maybe!" she said, her voice filled with awe and wonder as she looked into chocolate pools of adoration.

"Hmm, so what's taking so long?" Michelle grinned at her through the mirror.

"I was just savouring the moment." She kissed her shoulder, lightly leading her lips higher, up the length of her neck where she settled her attention just below an earlobe. Her fingers deftly tugged at the tiny hidden zip and separated the two sides of the dress, revealing the soft olive-toned skin to her touch. Michelle gasped as Cam lightly stroked her index finger down her spine. "I feel like a kid at Christmas that just keeps getting given the perfect gift."

Michelle twisted in her arms and shimmied, the dress falling away to reveal underwear Cam had definitely never seen before. "I hope you'll enjoy unwrapping me then."

In just their underwear, Cam grinned. Taking Michelle's hand, she turned and opened the door, tugging Michelle to follow her. "Cam! What are you doing?"

Cam brought a finger to her lips and shushed her.

"Don't shush me," Michelle argued, pulling back a little. She looked out and past Cam to make sure none of the staff where around to see them.

"Do you trust me?"

Michelle sagged slightly, her head tilting. "Of course I do."

"Then..." she tugged her hand again until she stepped forward. "Come on."

She led her wife along the narrow corridor towards the steps that led them back up to the deck. The breeze was welcome on their hot skin as carefully, Cam led them on a once-trodden route.

"Oh my God," she heard Michelle whisper as she caught sight of the bed. The same four poster bed they had first made love on. "Camryn, how?"

Before Cam could answer, the sound of an engine coming to life announced that the crew were leaving them. Only Gavin would stay aboard, and he had strict instructions not to come up on deck before sunrise.

"I just figured it was..."

"Perfect," Michelle finished for her. Her eyes found Cam's and held.

Cam nodded, drawn to her like a magnet. "Did I tell you today how much I love you?"

Michelle smiled. She knew just how much Camryn loved her, but she would play along anyway. "No," she rasped, arousal pumping through her system. She gasped as Cam reached around her and unhooked her bra. She let it fall to reveal herself.

"How remiss of me." Cam smiled, leaning in for a kiss. When she pulled away, she added, "I love you so much." Her hands slid down her sides, mapping her edges and the way that her hip bones jutted out just a little.

"I know."

Hooking into the lace panties, Cam pushed the material downward, until they dropped by themselves to the deck. Michelle stepped out of them. She shivered slightly in anticipation, much like she had that first night, when she hadn't been so sure of herself. Now, confidence rushed forth, urging her forwards as she stripped Cam of the last vestiges of cloth that separated them.

Naked, Michelle climbed up on the bed and waggled a come-hither finger in Cam's direction. Biting her lower lip as she watched the gorgeous woman that had just promised to spend her life with her, she almost forgot to close the curtains that would keep potential prying eyes from looking in on them.

She made light work of it, moving from one post to the next, undoing the ties that held each piece of material out of the way. They fell into place and the outside world was banished in an instant.

Cam took a breath and steadied herself, knowing that when she turned back around, her breath would be taken.

"Finally," Michelle complained with a smirk of amusement evident. She held her hand out and when Cam took it, she pulled hard, laughing as Cam landed on top of her. Their bodies pressed together, Cam giggled into her neck. When the laughing finally subsided, Cam raised up and looked down at her.

"Hi."

"Hey." Michelle caressed her cheek and felt Cam's pelvis grind down against her as the realisation of where they were, and why, hit home.

"I can't believe you are my wife," Cam whispered.

Michelle swallowed down the emotional lump that was building. "Well, I am, Mrs Thomas." Her hips rose up, connecting once more with the downward grind of her wife.

"Yeah, that sounds so...perfect." Her head tilted slightly as she leant down, pressing lips together, intimate and erotic as the kiss built to something more eager. Cam used her tongue to swipe gently across Michelle's lower lip. A request to enter, granted without thought. She took the opportunity to increase the pressure of her pelvis as they found a rhythm that suited the mood.

Water lapping at the side of the boat caused a gentle sway that was barely felt on the bed, not now that Cam was on the move. Her kisses marking the pathway they knew so well. Capturing a hardened nipple between her lips, she sucked and revelled in the soft moan of arousal that escaped Michelle's lips.

She always liked this bit best: watching Michelle come undone under her touch. Her fingertips explored, skimming, grasping, squeezing the flesh on offer to her. Her mouth was busy with kisses, licking and sucking, biting gently as she teased and coaxed Michelle's body to release. Only when Cam's fingers found the depth of her, sliding easily inside, her thrusts slow and powerful, did Michelle finally arch up and cry out.

Chapter Seven

Michelle surfaced from sleep first, tangled in bedclothes and her wife's limbs. She thought about that for a second: her wife. Just the words brought a smile to her lips. Then she lifted her left hand and caught the gleam of the new ring she was wearing.

"It's too early," Cam groaned as she opened one eye and caught a glimpse of her wife smiling at her.

"Hmm, really? It's too early?" Michelle asked as she rolled on top of her and pressed her pelvis against Cam's hard thigh, rocking into her with a slow tempo that she knew would arouse her.

"Yeah, way too early." Cam grinned as she flexed her quad muscle and gripped Michelle's hips, pressing her more firmly against the soft flesh that covered the hard, toned muscle she was currently working herself against.

"Tell me, Mrs Thomas, do you like being woken up early by your wife?"

"Love it," Cam groaned as her own arousal shot up at hearing Michelle call herself her wife. She tugged and pulled Michelle's thigh into her, pressing herself against her lover and riding out their climax together.

~Yes~

With no neighbours to annoy, the music was loud, and the newly installed lighting lit up the night sky with beams of light that shot around the dance floor, illuminating the joy. Their friends and family had come aboard earlier in the day after enjoying the most fabulous champagne breakfast. The day was warm and sunny as they took the yacht out to sea and enjoyed an afternoon of more champagne, great food, and wonderful company.

The kids ran around and pretended to be pirates while Robbie and Jen took the opportunity to let their hair down a little. With Martha and Bob onboard, it was the perfect time to let them enjoy some down time with the grandkids.

Members of cast and crew from *Medical Diaries* and other celebrity faces that Michelle was friendly with joined them later in the evening as the boat docked back in the harbour to allow those that needed to leave to get off, and those that were coming along to board.

Cam danced with her bride until her feet hurt and she felt blisters appearing, then she kicked off her shoes and danced some more. Her mother-in-law and father-in-law and then pretty much everyone else all lined up for their turn. Eventually she found a way of excusing herself to get another drink and came across Zac sitting quietly on the stairs. It was getting late, and she supposed he was probably tired.

"Hey Bud, what ya doing?" she asked as he looked up to see who was coming down the steps.

"Nothing much, just sitting," he replied. He looked cute in his miniature suit, though he had lost the jacket some time ago and now had his sleeves rolled up like his dad.

"I see, can I sit with you? I need a rest after all that dancing, they're killing me up there," she laughed. As soon as she had spoken, Zac began to cry and threw his arms around her. "Hey, hey, what's this all about?" she asked, pulling the young boy onto her lap to hold him properly.

"I thought you was going to die," he sobbed. His lower lip trembled as he pulled back to look at her. His eyes were glassy and filled with more tears, ready to spill over at any minute. Only his long, dark lashes held them at bay as he flopped back against her.

"You did?" she asked, and felt him nodding against her shoulder. "I'm sorry Zac, that you had to see what you did. You were such a brave boy."

"Mommy said that nasty lady hurt you." He looked up at her now, his big eyes wide and full of tears. She was livid with Jessica anyway, but now even more so, incensed that anyone would do something so monumentally horrifying in front of a child. But, right now she had to reign that anger in. Zac needed a calm auntie to help him.

"Yes, she did. She did something really ghastly, something that hurt me a lot and it made me very unwell, but I am okay now!"

"Really? You're really okay?"

"I am, I have some scars to prove it." She laughed and tickled him until he started to wriggle and grin.

"Can I see?"

"Uh maybe, not today though cos today is all about making Auntie Michelle happy, and she likes me in this suit and I'd have to take it off to show you my scars, but I will show you them another time if you still want to see them. Okay?"

He nodded, seemingly happy with that answer. "I'm going to get a drink," he said. "Want one?"

"I'm good Bud, but you go ahead." She watched as he turned and ran down to the bar area. She sat there a moment, just contemplating the conversation. She needed to help him move forward from this. It was her responsibility; it was because of her that Jessica had entered his life.

"You are truly amazing," said a welcome voice from the top of the stairs. Cam looked up and over her shoulder to see her wife walking down towards her. *Her wife, how good did that sound?* "I heard what you said to Zac," she said as she sat on Cam's knee, just like Zac had done.

"Eavesdropping already and married for less than a day, must be a record." Cam smiled, pressing a kiss to her lips.

"I think my wife is wonderful," Michelle gushed. Her arms slid easily around Cam's neck.

"Yes, but you are biased, so your opinion doesn't count," Cam replied, her own arms tightening their grip around her waist.

"My opinion is the *only* opinion that counts," she laughed.

"Hmm, I guess that is true. So, I am wonderful, huh?" she asked, kissing her wife again.

"More than wonderful really, but I don't want it to go to your head. I do have to live with you, after all."

Camryn roared with laughter. When she finally got her breath back, she let her eyes roam her wife's face, settling finally on her eyes. They were black as coal and filled with as much desire and want as her own.

"Do you think anyone would notice if we jumped ship and sailed away on the other boat?" Cam said quite seriously.

"We could, but I am actually enjoying myself, and now that I've managed to tie you down I can sneak away with you at any time for sex so, I think right now I will stay here and have you entertain me with more dancing." Their lips met once again.

"Ha, that's what I came down here to escape, your folks have worn me out."

"My folks, huh? Well, what if I promise not to let anyone else near you for the rest of the night and you only have to dance with me?"

"I might be persuaded."

Chapter Eight

Cam finally managed to carry Michelle over the threshold of their home on the third try, the first two attempts ending up with them both laughing too hard. Cam lost her balance and they collided with the wall.

Zac and Dylan both came running to the door to see what all the commotion was. "Don't drop Aunty 'Chelle, Cam," Dylan laughed.

"I'm trying not to, but she's a wriggler." Cam continued to chuckle.

Placing Michelle down onto her feet inside the threshold of their home, she instantly picked up Dylan instead and swung her around and into the air. The youngster squealed and giggled as Cam gently tossed her higher and then caught her.

"How you doing, shortstop?"

"You're funny," she chuckled before wriggling out of Cam's grip, running off the moment her feet hit the floor and Cam threatened the tickle monster.

It was Sunday evening, and the entire family was gathered for dinner before they headed back home. It had been such a busy and exciting weekend, and they were grateful for a more tranquil few hours.

Jen and Michelle sat together on the couch chatting about the wedding and how beautiful it was. Michelle was happily showing off her ring to pretty much anyone that showed an interest. Martha was busy in the kitchen cooking up something that smelt so absolutely fantastic that it was making Cam's stomach rumble.

Robbie and Bob were talking golf out on the veranda. She could hear the low timber of their voices as they spoke to one another. It was nice to look around and finally feel like her house was a home.

Dylan had fallen asleep on Michelle's lap with her wife's fingers lazily brushing through the flaxen hair, tenderly like a mother would. Cam spent a few moments just watching the scene before she felt eyes on her.

She turned a little towards where she felt the stare was coming from and found Zac, sitting by himself on the floor, just looking at her.

Cam narrowed her eyes at him and smiled before asking, "You okay, Bud?"

He nodded his head slowly, but continued to stare. Cam stood and walked over to him. He watched her the entire way. Michelle and Jen stopped talking in order to observe the pair as Cam dropped down to her haunches, putting herself on his level.

"Do you want to see them?" she asked him, knowing full well that he knew what she meant. He nodded his head again. Cam turned to Jen and smiled. "Zac would like to look at my scars to make sure I am okay, is that alright with you?"

Jen nodded and Cam stood, holding her hand out for Zac. He reached up and took it. His hand looked so small in her grasp, and she realised even more so at just how young he was. She took a deep breath and sighed deeply before smiling down at him and leading him towards the door so they could go somewhere a little more private.

"Is it ok if I..." Jen didn't need to finish her sentence as Cam nodded and smiled.

"Of course."

Martha came out from the kitchen and watched the small group follow each other up the stairs.

"What's going on?" she asked Michelle, whose fingers were still teasing through Dylan's hair as she slept.

"I believe it's an impromptu therapy session for Zac...and Cam."

~Yes~

Once inside the room, Cam closed the door and flicked on the light. Then sitting Zac on the edge of the bed, she knelt in front of him.

"So, do you know why I have these scars?" she asked gently, watching as he nodded.

"Because the nasty lady hurt you." He watched his mother as she moved around them to come sit on the bed beside him.

"That's right, and when she did, well she hurt something inside of me that meant the doctors had to do an operation to fix it." Cam explained.

"What kind of operation?" he asked. Jen remained quiet. She had nothing to add at this point; what she did know what that Zac needed this. He had questions he was afraid to ask anyone, but he would ask Cam. They would share this connection always.

"Do you know what your lungs do?"

"Yes," he nodded. "They're what make you breathe."

"Yep, that's right, you are very smart!" Cam smiled. "So, when Jessica got angry she-"

"Jessica?" he asked, interrupting her.

"Yes, the nasty lady is called Jessica." She wanted him to know her name, to realise she was just a person and not a scary monster or nasty lady that would haunt him.

"Okay."

"So, when Jessica hurt me, she caused an injury to my lung, and that meant the doctors had to operate to fix it. They are like balloons that blow up when we breathe in, and mine had a puncture, so when I breathed in it didn't work, and because of that my heart got very ill, does that make sense?"

"Yes," he replied solemnly.

"Okay, so I wanted to tell you that so that when you see my scar you won't be worried about why I have it, because it's quite big and can look a bit scary but it's really not, it just looks like it."

"Okay." He looked at her and then down to her chest, waiting.

With that, Cam took a deep breath and lifted her t-shirt up over her head. She stayed knelt on the floor in just her bra and shorts and allowed Zac to look at her for a moment, then she slowly showed him each one of the stab wounds, letting him reach out and run his small finger across each one.

"Do they hurt?" His touch was gentle; some he barely touched, others he examined more closely.

"No not really, sometimes they ache a little bit, but they don't hurt. Actually, I can't feel some of them."

"This one looks like a Z," he said, pointing. Cam looked down at the scar just under her arm and laughed.

"You're right, Shall I call it Zac?"

He nodded and smiled. Then he drew his tiny fingers down the scar in the centre of her chest. Tears formed in her eyes, and he quickly pulled his hand away, thinking he had hurt her.

"No, it's not you," she said, taking his hand and placing it back on the scar. "Sometimes I just get tearful, but it isn't because of you or because it hurts, okay?"

"Okay." He looked to his mom for reassurance, and she smiled and nodded at him. She too had been near to tears watching them both go through this unscheduled therapy session together. She knew Zac had been withdrawn since the incident with Cam. Robbie and she hadn't been able to find a way through with him because he didn't want to talk about it. So, if he wanted to talk to Cam, then so be it.

"Anything else you want to ask me?" Cam said, watching him watching her. He thought for a moment, unsure if he could ask what he wanted to. "You can ask me anything," she reassured him.

"Did you...did you die?" His eyes were cloudy as he blinked back the tears that threatened to spill over once again.

Cam looked to Jen for permission to go into more detail with him. She nodded in reply, smiling at Cam. If they were going to get through this, then they needed to be honest with him as much as possible.

"Hmm well, I guess I did, yes, but not for very long. My heart was under a lot of pressure because I couldn't breathe properly and twice it stopped beating, but the doctors fixed it very fast, so I was okay again," she reiterated quickly, seeing the frown on his face that threatened to erupt into something more.

"Did you see God?" he asked quickly.

Cam smiled and tried to hold back a chuckle. It was actually very sweet that he thought she would be going up and not down. "No, I don't think I was there long enough to go to Heaven."

"That's good... I didn't want you to die!"

"Well I didn't want to die either, that's why I fought very hard to stay alive."

"And you're really okay now?"

"Yep, though I'm a little cold, can I put my tee back on?" she said with a giggle. He giggled too and nodded furiously.

"So, anything else ya wanna know?" He shook his head and so she smiled at him and ruffled his hair. "Wanna go get some dinner now?" Cam asked, and he nodded his head.

"Yeah, I'm starving," he said, jumping up and throwing his arms around Cam, "Thank you."

As he ran out of the room to go find Grandma and see how long till dinner, Jen stopped Cam. "Thank you, Cam, he has been withdrawn since, ya know," she said, not sure what to say about it.

"I figured he needed to talk about it." She seemed to spend a lifetime talking about it, much of it against her own wishes, but she understood the benefits of getting it all out. And if that's what Zac needed from her, then she would be there.

"Yeah, I think he saw much more than he lets on, and I know it bothers him. He's a good kid and he takes a lot of things to heart."

"He can talk to me anytime he needs to, if you're okay with that. What about Dylan?"

"Sure, I think he would like that too. Dyl seems fine, I'm not sure she really understood what happened, but if that changes..." Jen smiled and hugged her tight. "We're family, right?"

"Yes, we definitely are."

Chapter Nine

Falling into bed that night, comfortably wrapped in each other's arms, felt like the best feeling in the world. They had spent the day lounging around the house with just a few excursions for some amorous exercise in the bedroom. Keeping their hands off of one another had become even more difficult.

Cam took a moment to study this woman who was now her wife. She was flawless in Cam's eyes; nothing about her could ever be replaced by anyone else. She was exquisite, and every moment spent in her presence was never enough. When she pressed their lips together she felt that electricity spark through her veins and hit her straight at her core. There was never a time it failed to happen. From just a kiss, it would ignite a passion that she had no doubts about.

She rolled up and over, balancing herself on her palms above the supine brunette. Her eyesight catching the gleam of the ring she now wore made her smile inwardly before it burst forth and settled on her features. She was happy as she leant forwards and captured waiting lips, taking her time to enjoy the softness before she kissed a trail along the strong jawline.

"I fall in love with you again every day," Cam said as she began a familiar descent down the valley of her wife's chest toward the toned abdomen that awaited – muscles that quivered and tensed with the knowledge of what was to come.

"Hold up." Michelle stopped her. "Back up here, please."

Cam did as she was requested and took another moment to focus on those pools of molten chocolate that were looking at her right now, falling ever deeper into them. She wanted to drown in them and then be rescued just so she could drown again.

"Hmm?"

"Say that again."

Cam's gaze moved from Michelle's eyes to her lips and then back again, falling into them over and over as she said once more, "I fall in love with you again every day."

Michelle held her gaze and then said something she never imagined she would ever utter and had never even considered before this exact moment. "I want to have our baby." Once she said it out loud, she realised it was exactly what she wanted, what she had always wanted and had just accepted she couldn't have.

"What?" Cam laughed and moved to straddle her in order to be more comfortable, more grounded. She searched her face for any sign that this was a joke, but found none. "You're serious?"

Michelle had laughed too at first; it was absurd, but now she was quite serious as she nodded. "Yeah, I think so."

Cam took in those beautiful eyes once more, those eyes that looked at her with nothing other than adoration. And she imagined a life growing inside of her, a perfect, healthy little life that they could create together. "I wanna say yes." She sat up properly and tried to gather her thoughts, staring up at the ceiling – anywhere but into those eyes that were filled with excitement and now fear, fear that Cam would say no.

"But?" Michelle probed hesitantly; she had been so sure that Cam would agree. Something deep inside told her this was the right thing to do, for both of them, but maybe she was wrong. Maybe she had gotten it wrong.

Cam turned to look at her. Shrugging, she said, "I dunno, I just...I never considered it being an option before." She turned away again and this time, she stared at the floor. "I'm not sure I'm great parent material."

"Wow, really?" Michelle chuckled, "Have you seen the way my niece and nephew love you?"

"Yeah, but that's not on a daily basis, they go home to people that make decisions for them. We just get the fun part," she explained.

Michelle pressed her lips together and blinked back the tears. "You're right, it was a stupid suggestion."

"No, no it's not stupid," Cam blurted. "I'm not saying no. God, I can't imagine anything more beautiful than you carrying our child. It's just, we literally just got married, and it's been such a whirlwind. I want to enjoy it, enjoy us." She grasped Michelle's hands. "I know that sounds selfish-"

"It's not, I want that too...I just, I'm putting it out there that one day I wanna have a baby with you." She leant forward and kissed the edge of Cam's mouth. "But we can do a lot of practicing first."

"Yeah, we can definitely do that." Cam laughed as she was pulled back into an embrace.

Chapter Ten

With four weeks left until Michelle was required back on set for season 14 of *Medical Diaries,* it was the perfect opportunity for them to get away on honeymoon. Cam had wanted to book them on an uninhabited island someplace hot where they could just be together, make love, and enjoy nobody trying to kill them. Michelle, on the other hand, wanted to do something a little more straightforward. She wanted to go to England and see where Cam grew up.

"Oh man, really? You do know I left there for a reason, don't you?" Cam argued from her seat behind the desk. It was still early in the day and she was catching up on paperwork while the staff got ready for the late afternoon and early evening rush.

"Yes, and she is currently locked up awaiting trial, so I really don't see why you are so against it," Michelle reasoned from her seat by the window.

"But, wouldn't you rather lie on a beach all day and do bugger all?" Cam asked. "Practice making that baby we talked about?"

"I can do that every day, why would I want to do it on vacation?" she argued back, taking a sip of her drink. She crossed her legs, her skirt rising up a little to show off a firm thigh that had Cam's attention.

"Honeymoon!!" Cam reminded her. "That means we won't leave the hotel anyway, so we might as well be on an island!" she said, thinking she had won the argument.

"However, we are going to have a child one day, and I want to be able to tell him or her everything they ever want to know about both their mommas. So, book us a vacation to England or…"

"Or?" Cam asked, turning slowly and narrowing her eyes at Michelle.

Michelle sat forward and rested her elbows on her knees as she replied, "Or you will be finding out what not touching my body feels like."

Cam stopped moving, her arm half way to her mouth with her drink. "That is so unfair."

"Maybe so," she answered with a smirk.

"You can't keep using sex as a way to get me to do your bidding, lady," Cam stated, finally taking a swig of her drink.

"Oh, I think I can." She winked. Standing up, she smoothed out the wrinkles in her skirt and moved around the room towards where Cam sat.

"Fine, I'll take you to England." Her lips twitched at the corners. "I might just leave you there," she said trying not to grin. She really needed to try and find a way to not just give in to her wife's demands, but she feared that was something she would never learn to do. It might be easier to just accept it.

"Thank you, baby," Michelle said as she leant in, warm lips pressed against Cam's cheek. "Wanna go get some lunch?"

"Yes! But I must book flights to England, so I am too busy," she said raising an eyebrow in jest.

"Aww, well I can go and get something for you if you would like?" Michelle offered, her finger twirling lazily in her hair.

"So kind, but I wouldn't want to put you to any trouble," Cam countered, "Anyway, I'm not that hungry."

"No?" Michelle said suggestively as she nudged Cam's thighs apart and moved between them. Cam sat back in her chair watching. "Maybe if you checked out the menu you might find something that takes...your...fancy," she said, slowly lifting her skirt and slipping her panties down her thighs, not once taking her eyes from Camryn's ice blues. Her favourite thing in the world was watching those darken with desire.

"Well, it never hurts to look," Cam countered. She wasn't sure there would ever be a time when she would turn down an offer like that from her wife

Michelle leant back against the desk and lifted her left leg to balance a heel on the arm of Cam's chair. Cam continued to watch, waiting for the right leg to follow suit and find its place, pinning Cam in place. Once it did she grabbed a hold of both ankles and pulled her chair in closer. "I just realised, we never did finish what we started on this desk that first night we met." Cam signalled her to lift. With her butt lifted, Cam pushed the material higher, revealing all she had to offer.

"Hmm that's true, long overdue I would say, wouldn't you?" Michelle gasped as Cam found her in an instant. Without pause, she tantalised her and teased her into ecstasy. Her tongue did things to Michelle that would liquify her very soul. Her hips undulated and reared upwards, an urgency seeping through her. Glancing down she locked eyes with Cam. There was nothing more erotic than watching as Cam took her time to pleasure her like this. She felt that all-too-familiar sensation as her tummy coiled, her climax forcing its way to the fore, and she collapsed backwards. Her thighs tightened and gripped, ankles crossed, holding Cam in place until she could take no more and she released her with a contented gasp.

~Yes~

Flights were easy enough to organise, and she already had somewhere in mind to stay when they got there. Now that she thought about it, the opportunity to check on things back in the UK made a lot of sense. She sent emails off to the relevant people telling them to expect her.

With Michelle gone, she bounded down the stairs in search of Erin. She didn't need permission to leave for a couple of weeks, but she did need to make sure everything was covered and organised, out of politeness if nothing else!

"Erin, are you ok with me just buggering off for a couple of weeks?" Cam asked, spotting the bleach blonde head with pink tips that bobbed behind the bar as she searched for something on a shelf.

"Huh? Yeah sure," she said, her head popping up to see where the voice came from.

"What ya looking for?" Cam reached down for a beer, popped the lid and took a swig.

"Uh, a flyer...for a band...they were looking for a gig and I thought it might be something different to offer on a Thursday?" She stood and grinned at her boss.

Cam considered the idea. Live music hadn't been something she had considered previously, but now she thought about it. "Sounds like a plan. Okay, I'll leave you to organise that. We will be jetting off in the next day or so."

"Alright, have fun!" Erin offered a wink along with the grin. "Which of course, I am sure you will, seeing as it's your honeymoon."

"Yeah, being dragged back to my hometown is not my idea of fun...but, it's what she wants so..." Cam shrugged.

"Whipped," Erin quipped, grinning at her boss.

She downed the rest of the drink and expertly tossed the bottle into the recycle bin before returning to her office. "Ya know, I think I am."

~Yes~

The last thing she needed to do was speak with Gavin. It had never sat well with her having to have bodyguards and be followed around everywhere she went, and now, with Jessica's arrest, she wanted to get back to some normality around the place.

"So, Michelle and I will be heading to London," she said as soon as Gavin had entered the room. He sat down in the chair opposite her and nodded.

"Okay, I'll make arrangements for..."

She cut him off quickly. "No, that's what I wanted to talk to you about. I don't want anyone coming with us. There's no need."

"Alright. So, what do you want me to do? Organise someone over there?"

She shook her head and smiled at his confusion. "No, I just want to take my wife on honeymoon. And while we're gone, I'd like you to reorganise the staff. Keep Carrie, Henry, and Jorge on if they want to stay. It makes sense to have a small team available, but we don't need-"

"I get it, Cam. Jessica is not a problem now, and unless there is any credible threat then it makes sense to lighten the staff. It was never a permanent position, most of the guys are expecting to move on at some point anyway."

Relieved, she sat back in her chair. "Good, so listen, pay everyone till the end of next month."

"Sure, and I'll see you in a couple of weeks?" he asked as he stood up to leave.

"That you will."

Chapter Eleven

The plane touched down at Heathrow on time, and while it was just about still daylight, it felt like the middle of the night to the weary travellers. Trying not to yawn, Cam followed Michelle as she led the way towards Car Hire. Cam had pre-paid to pick up a vehicle. They loaded up and got on the road as quickly as they could. Cam drove of course, she knew the roads, and she was used to the wrong side as Michelle consistently argued.

The drive into London was horrendous. Traffic was a problem anywhere in the world at rush hour, but for a city as small as London, it was even more suffocating as they wound their way around to the M4 and the virtually straight route through.

Michelle was busy looking out of the window at all the green fields they were passing. She noticed the temperature on the dashboard, 14 degrees. No wonder it was so cold. Cam was explaining each area as they passed. Chiswick and then through Hammersmith. It was all a little dull until Cam said Hyde Park, and then before they knew it, they were passing Buckingham Palace and then they were crossing the river. That was when she noticed the MI6 building from the James Bond movie and squealed a little with excitement. Cam grinned.

They were sitting in traffic as they crossed Vauxhall Bridge, passing the iconic building, the traffic lights taking an age to change from red to green.

"I meant to tell you." She glanced to her left at Michelle. "I arranged to see Jo, she manages the bar I own here, Art," she reminded Michelle as they started moving again.

"Seriously? How long is that going to take?" Michelle turned in her seat and glared incredulously at her. "This is our honeymoon, Cam. You're supposed to leave work behind."

"I know, but it just seemed pointless coming all this way and not stopping in to check on things."

Michelle huffed. "Is it like OUT?" she asked as the car came to another slow halt. The traffic in the inside lane seemed to be moving a lot quicker, and she wondered why Cam didn't get into that one and get them moving.

"Not really, it's much smaller. Its more eclectic that OUT. It's got a dancefloor though!" she said, hopeful that the idea of music and a night out might entice Michelle to be a little happier about it.

"So, we can make a night of it, then?" Michelle asked, casting a sideways glance at Cam. It felt strange sitting in the wrong seat.

"Yeah, if you like, you can still get hot and sweaty with me," she grinned. The lights turned green, and Cam followed the traffic and turned right.

~Yes~

Her apartment, or flat as she called it, was in an executive high-rise block on the banks of the Thames. She parked the car in her allotted space and climbed out. Michelle followed and waited for Cam to pull the cases from the boot. She wondered why it was called a boot and not a trunk, but Cam hadn't known the answer. She took the smaller carry-on cases and wheeled them towards the elevator, or lift. That she could understand; it lifted them up. Cam followed, pulling the larger cases behind her. They rode upwards for what didn't feel very long at all, and yet, they had reached the top.

The penthouse.

The views from there were amazing; you could see for miles in every direction and from every room. It was wall-to-wall windows on two sides in each room you entered. It was bright and airy and modern. Everything about it screamed superior.

Michelle shrieked as she ran from room to room. "Oh my God, I can see the Houses of Parliament!"

Cam came up behind her to look down the river towards the historic building. "Just to the left, that's Westminster Abbey and across the river, you can just see it, that's the London Eye. I booked us tickets to go on it. It's in Southbank, I think you'll love it there. Lots of cool restaurants and things to do."

Michelle turned and threw her arms around Cam's neck. "I am going to love everything, just because I'm here with you."

"Well, duh." Cam laughed. "Of course you are."

"What else have you planned?" she said, leaning up and kissing her.

Cam smiled and looked out across the river again before her eyes were drawn back to Michelle. "So many plans..."

Michelle laughed. "Other than getting me naked, which by the way, I am very happy with."

"Well, once we get over the jetlag, I was thinking we could jump on a river taxi and head down to Tower Bridge... and then we can go to..."

"Tower Bridge?!! Oh my God, and the Tower of London, right, we're going to go there too, right?"

"Okay, Miss Excitable, maybe you shouldn't have had that last shot of coffee."

Michelle playfully slapped Cam's shoulder. "I am excited to be here. It's where you're from, and anything about you...excites me."

"Ya know, if I wasn't so tired right now..." As if on cue, she yawned. "I'd let you show me just how excited by me you are!"

~Yes~

Waking up the following morning after a ten-hour sleep, Michelle got up and made a cup of coffee. While Cam slept, she wandered the apartment and tried to get a feel for the Camryn that once lived here.

There were photographs on the walls. Michelle examined them closer and noted that they were each signed with C.T. *Had Cam taken these? If so, then why had she never seen her with a camera?*

As she scoured the room looking at all the other little items that gave her further insight into the Camryn from before they met, she noted a framed picture of a man and a woman, maybe early sixties. The woman was blonde like Cam, but where Cam's face was open and honest, this woman's face looked sad, even though she was smiling.

There were a few ornaments and some books but nothing else; it was as though she had never gotten around to finishing things here.

"Ah, there you are!" Cam exclaimed, coming up behind her to wrap strong arms around her middle.

"Here I am." Michelle smiled, enjoying the closeness of her. It was something she would never tire of. Being in her wife's arms meant a safety she had never felt before.

"Did you want to go out or hang around here and chill?" Cam stifled another yawn. She was tired still; she never could get used to these time differences, but at least she had gotten a good night's sleep. It was just after seven in the morning. A grey sky full of clouds outside reminded her she was home. *Home* a word that sounded so unfamiliar back here. She caught sight of her wedding ring and realised that home was now just anywhere Michelle was.

"Hmm I don't mind, what do you want to do?"

"I want to go to an island in the sunshine, but alas I am here, in the middle of March, and the only brightness to that is that you are here too." She smiled and kissed her cheek.

"Did you take these pictures?" Michelle asked, pointing out the large frames that hung in front of them.

"Yes." Michelle felt Cam nod against her shoulder as her arms tensed around her waist.

"They're really good, why haven't I seen you with a camera?"

"Because I don't take photographs anymore," Cam said quickly. Her arms fell to her side and she took a step backwards, away from the images.

Michelle turned to her, she smiled. "Clearly, but why not? You're very good at it."

Cam took a deep breath, reached out her hand, and when Michelle took it, she led her to the couch, sitting rather awkwardly so she could look at her properly. Cam sighed and grimaced as she decided what she wanted to say. Her arms folded across her chest as she spoke. "My dad taught me, it was our thing." She sounded sad and Michelle wanted to hold her, but she wasn't sure that was what Camryn needed right now. "And now he doesn't speak to me, so I just don't do it anymore."

Now that Michelle thought about it, she realised that Cam had never really mentioned her family. She mentally slapped herself for not thinking to ask. It was only when Cam was in hospital that Michelle had thought about them. She had taken Cam's mobile phone and scrolled through the address book looking for a "Mum," but there wasn't one listed. She had checked for "parents," "home," and all the other alternatives for the words "Mum" and "Dad," but all she found was a Caroline Thomas. She had left messages and sent texts, but never heard a reply, and then she had forgotten all about it as she sat, night after night, at Cam's bedside. She had assumed they would meet while they were in London, that Cam would invite her home to meet the family.

"Why doesn't he speak to you?" she probed gently.

"I'm a disappointment to him," Cam said bitterly, her gaze turned towards the skyline as she continued. "They have never accepted my being gay, it wasn't allowed to be mentioned. I couldn't introduce them to any of my girlfriends and I certainly wasn't allowed to do anything that would give cause for neighbours and family to find out."

"That must have been very hard to live with," Michelle consoled.

"I was 17, and all I had in the world was them and my sister Caroline. She was at work though. She left the minute she could to go to Uni and then got a job, and I couldn't blame her for that, but I hated her for it too. So, I was stuck with them until I finished my college course."

Michelle frowned. There really was so much they didn't know about each other. "What did you study?"

"Business studies, it was pretty boring but it's helped a lot I guess."

Michelle nodded. "So, what did you do after college?"

"Moved out and into a flat-share with 5 friends. It was the most freeing moment of my life, finally I could just be me. I only saw my parents for holidays and birthdays and even then, if I could avoid it I would."

"I wish I had known you back them."

"You don't," she laughed. "I was quite dull. But I was happy, I met lots of new people and started to gain confidence. I made a life that was separate from them. They were my folks and I had girlfriends, and never the twain shall meet, or so they say. And that was fine for years until I met..." She paused, a scowl turning into a thin-lipped rueful smile. "Well then I met Jessica and I wanted them to meet her, I was going to be living with her, so she was important. My mum wasn't really the problem, it was my dad that had issues with it, but she...I guess she didn't know how to have a mind of her own and so she just went along with it – a quiet life I suppose."

"That's just so sad."

"Yeah. When I took Jess home to meet them I hoped that maybe they had gotten used to the idea by now; it had been years since I'd come out. But no, he threw us out, told me I was never to darken his door again unless I could bring a suitable man home and not someone wanting to be one. And I never spoke to them again until I won all that money. I sent them a cheque, I don't know why but I figured my karma didn't have to plummet, they were...are my parents, and I wanted them to be comfortable, and so I sent them a cheque for £3 million. I got a phone call the following day telling me that no amount of money would make a difference, that I needed to just stop messing around and grow up." She laughed and shook her head. "I had to grow up?" she repeated, pointing to herself.

"What did you do?"

"I put the phone down and cancelled the cheque."

"You did not!" Michelle laughed and placed her hand to her mouth in shock.

"I did. I thought ya know what, fuck you!"

"What did you do with the money?"

"I set up an LGBT charity with it and named it after him. The Ronald Thomas LGBT Support Group meets every Wednesday in our local community centre." They both burst into laughter at that. "I even paid for great big banners and posters to go up around town. Childish, I know." She chuckled at the memory. Michelle fell quiet and looked to the floor guiltily. "What is it?"

"I have a confession, something I completely forgot about until now," she admitted. She smiled at her wife and reached for her. Cam accepted her hand instantly. "When you were in the hospital...after..." She paused, knowing Cam knew what she was talking about "I...well I didn't know if you would survive and I...I thought it was the right thing to do." She floundered a little.

"Babe just say it, I'm not going to be angry about anything you did during that period." Cam linked their fingers and squeezed them gently.

"I called your sister," Michelle blurted, wincing at the idea that she might have inadvertently caused Cam a problem.

"Oh, okay, well I can assume from the lack of visitation that she didn't pass the message on?" Cam tried to laugh off the hurt, but Michelle felt it just as much. She couldn't imagine going through something like that and not having her own mother by her bedside. It was no wonder that Cam looked to Maria for maternal love.

"I checked your phone and found a number. I didn't know what else to do. God forbid if it were ever me, then I'd wanna know, and so I called, but it always went into voicemail. I left several messages, but now I realise that she never called back."

"And now you understand why I don't talk about them much?"

"Sadly, I do. My poor baby, why didn't you tell me?"

Cam shrugged, "Because I don't think about them much. Coming back here though...I guess it's going to bring some things up." She smiled and got comfortable on the couch, tugging Michelle to sit with her, to lie against her chest so she could hold her.

"I'm sorry, I guess I didn't think about how coming back here would make you feel," Michelle all but whispered. Cam kissed the top of her head. She wanted to continue with her story.

"I won all that money and left within days of it. I settled quickly in LA, but I came back here after 3 months cos of visa issues. While I was here I bought this place. It was empty, they were still finishing off the build. I stayed a month, contemplated whether to go back to the States or not. I put the word out that I was here. I know my parents knew, but neither of them bothered to contact me and so that made my mind up. I went back to the States as soon as I could and found my home."

"Did you make it known you would be back this time?"

She shook her head, "No, the only person here that knows is Jo. I'm sure she has warned the staff to be on best behaviour, but nobody that knows my parents," she explained.

"So, what about your sister? Do you speak to her?"

"Yeah, but she works for the government. I don't even know what she does, it's all hush hush apparently, and she is always away from home. The last time I spoke to her she was in Hong Kong, and that was a year ago."

"So, you're not close then?"

"I thought we were, but..." she shrugged. "She's 7 years older than me. I was the annoying little sister. We're not like you and Robbie." She chuckled. "We don't dislike each other, but she has her life and I have mine and they rarely clash."

"I'd like to meet her one day," Michelle said, her voice quiet and thoughtful, Cam kissed the side of her head. "If you want me to." She twisted so she could look up at Cam and placed a gentle kiss on her chin.

"Yeah, maybe. If she ever has time for me," Cam added. Melancholy wrapped her words.

~Yes~

Condensation dripped down the window, a combination of the heating system and the heat being generated in the bed. The duvet was discarded, hanging off the bed, and the sheets were tangled around them both. Cam lay on her back an arm flung across her forehead as she caught her breath. Slick with sweat, she felt her lover roll into her side and rest her cheek against her chest.

"Why am I never satisfied? I could take you over and over and over and still want more of you," Cam whispered into the darkness, the night sky obscured with black clouds only helping to make the room feel darker. Michelle squeezed her arm tighter around Cam's waist. They'd gone to bed to sleep, only to find jet lag had other ideas.

"I don't know, but I feel that way too. I am never fully relaxed without you near me, touching me. It's like I need to be physically connected to you at all times and when I can't be, then I need to gorge myself on you to make it last through the barren times I know might come."

"Wow, that's, that's kind of hot," Cam said instantly feeling herself clench at Michelle's words. She rolled over to face her, nose to nose almost. "I have a fantasy," she admitted.

"Really?" Michelle leant up on one arm now, intrigued by this news. She always enjoyed it when Cam came up with something new. She reminded herself to start thinking about her own fantasies to share with Cam.

"Yep," she replied, nodding slowly, a shy grin appearing on her face as she thought about it. "But, I'm not sure..." she glanced back out of the window.

"Tell me, you know I'll make all your dreams come true, Camryn," Michelle whispered against her ear seductively. Cam couldn't hold back the moan that escaped with the way Michelle said her name, almost sending her over the edge again. "It is our honeymoon after all."

She took a moment to get her libido back under control. When she could finally speak, she said, "Well. I've always wanted to...with someone up against that window." She nodded towards the large window in front of them. An eyebrow raised along with the smirk that started to lift the corner of her mouth, the same corner that Michelle kissed before she turned and looked towards the windows in the room. They were 32 floors up and it was almost 4 am. The chances of anyone being able to see them were minute, but the idea that someone could, well, that was exciting, wasn't it? It still amazed her at just how much more enthusiastic she was about sex and trying new things than she had been with previous partners.

She sat up and let the sheet fall away from her body as she reached for Cam's hand and led her out of the bed. They padded naked across the cool floor, with Michelle walking backwards pulling Camryn along with her. She had that predatory look in her eye that Cam couldn't get enough of

When they reached the tall windows, Michelle pulled Cam closer and kissed her. Her lips nipped and teased at her lover's mouth until finally, unable to hold back any longer, Cam joined her in deepening the kiss.

"Tell me what you fantasise about." Michelle's voice was silky and had dropped at least one octave as she spoke against Cam's ear. Camryn swallowed as goosebumps rose from her flesh, arousal now pouring through her veins at a rate of knots she hadn't known before.

Cam lavished her neck with kisses, her tongue sweeping upwards. "Well, in my fantasy, the woman...you, you're standing with your palms..." Michelle didn't wait for further instructions. She turned and placed her hands against the glass.

She glanced over her shoulder at Camryn. "Like this?" Her voice was breathy and seductive.

"Yeah, just like that," Cam answered, her chest heaving as she moved in behind her, grasping Michelle's hips. Fingertips skimmed the surface of her ribcage before moving more firmly to take her breasts in her grasp. She teased the flesh and pushed herself against Michelle, hips undulating against the soft skin of Michelle's butt.

Cam's chin rested lightly on Michelle's right shoulder. Michelle she could feel Cam's hot breath against her cheek. She arched into Cam's palm as her right hand shifted and began to move, lying flush against her abdomen as it journeyed towards her centre. She closed her eyes and concentrated on the feeling of Cam's lips as they connected with her neck. She gasped when talented digits made a gentle intrusion between her folds, gliding effortlessly through the abundant wetness to stroke her, back and forth. The connection between them was electric. She felt her pulse race as her body tried to keep pace.

Michelle arched again, her backside pressing into Cam as she felt herself begin to surrender to the ever-growing sensations developing deep within her. Sensations that would erupt the moment Cam eased her over the edge.

She was so engrossed in her pleasure, she was surprised when she felt Cam twist her around, pushing her backwards until her back hit the cold glass. Cam claimed her mouth with her own, entering her at the same time, working her up into another frenzy, pushing her towards that precipice. She hooked her leg around Cam's waist and clawed at her back in an effort to pull her deeper, harder, faster. When Cam cried out at the sharp pain, it only propelled her further.

It was erotic and daring, the prospect of being caught only adding to her arousal as the whole of London slept on unaware. Michelle felt herself constrict and she tried to relax, to hold it off just a little longer. Cam had felt it too and found her with her eyes. They held like that, darkened with lust as they battled an almost silent need to win. Cam grunted with the effort, needing to take Michelle to highs she had never flown before, but her wife wanted something more. So, she eased off, accepted the unspoken invitation to make this last, to draw it out and let Michelle dictate when she would be satisfied. The thought that this had now changed from *her* fantasy to *theirs* made her even more determined to give Michelle everything she ever asked for.

Finally, it was too much. Neither could fight it any longer. Michelle grabbed Cam's face, holding her right there as she fought to keep her eyes open and hold Cam's gaze, completely overwhelmed by the feelings between her thighs. Her wife's fingers deep inside her and then finally, Cam's thumb pressed against her clitoris. She gave in and succumbed to her.

Chapter Twelve

It was difficult to move around without being jostled, and Michelle clung onto Cam's arm for dear life as they dodged in and out of the traffic to cross the road. Grey skies continued to lurk up above, but the vibrant colour of jackets, hats, and scarves worn by tourists and locals as they flittered around the imposing column in the centre of Trafalgar Square was much more appealing.

Cam had found her old camera, and after much cajoling from Michelle, she had slung it around her neck and promised to take some photos while they were out and about. If she was honest, it had been fun. Michelle was happy to pose just about anywhere she asked. They took selfies with their phones and posted them to social media. Erin clicked "like" within seconds,

Cam chuckled. "Ya think she ever puts her phone down?"

Michelle grinned over her shoulder and looked at the picture of them both, standing in front of one of the huge lions that guarded the corners of the Admiral's perch. "Nope. Cute pic though."

"Yeah, well you're in it," Cam joked. The counter for likes was changing every second as fans of Michelle started to find the photograph. "See, all your fans are following me now."

"Oh, I am sure a few of them are actually following you."

"If you say so, but before I met you, I had like 40 followers. Now, there's thousands of them." She laughed as she looked up and caught someone taking their photograph. "Come on, there is more to see."

Grabbing her hand, she led Michelle away from the square and up some steps. A large building loomed up in front of them. More columns and a small dome. Red banners swung downwards and fluttered in the breeze, The National Gallery printed clearly in white. It wasn't exactly Cam's favourite place to wander around, but she liked a few of the paintings that hung there. Michelle though, she was in her element, dragging Cam from one room to the next. When they stood in front of the famous "Sunflowers" by Vincent Van Gogh, she was visibly moved. The story of the Dutch artist had been one she had read about at school.

"I had a print of this on my wall for years," she explained as Cam looked at it and tried to see what was so interesting about it.

"Uh huh."

Noticing Cam's lack of interest, she leant in and whispered, "He cut off his own ear."

Aghast, Cam turned to her. "Why?"

Michelle shrugged. "Nobody really knows, they say he went mad." She pushed her arm through Cam's and pulled her close. "Come on, take me somewhere else then...somewhere more exciting that you can take photographs of."

"Back to the apartment then?" she grinned, waggling her eyebrows suggestively. "And naked, right?"

~Yes~

They walked the straight path to the Mall, under Admiralty Arch, towards Buckingham Palace. "The Queen is home," she said, pointing to a flag that blew in the breeze from the top of the building.

"How can you tell?"

"Because that's the Royal Standard, it only flies when the Queen is in residence. Otherwise it would just be the Union flag."

"The Union Jack?"

Cam made a face. "Kind of, its only called the Union Jack when it's flown by a ship, otherwise, it's just the Union Flag." She had heard that in a pub quiz and remembered it.

"Oh...So, we can't go in?" Michelle pouted, ignoring Cam's piece of useless information.

Cam shook her head. "Nah, it's only open to public for two months of the year, and only when the Queen isn't here. I checked earlier online."

They joined the group of people all standing around the gates, waiting their turn to have their photograph taken in front of the palace. Cam snapped a few shots of Michelle and then jumped in with her and took a few selfies with her phone. Erin clicked like instantly.

"Jeez, I need to keep her busier." She laughed. "I'm starving. Let's get some grub."

A black cab passed, and Cam threw out an arm just too late. She didn't worry about it though; another taxi soon headed their way and they jumped in. "Southbank, please."

~Yes~

The London Eye loomed up high above them as they walked hand in hand along the embankment, a giant wheel slowly turning 32 capsules filled with people that wanted to view London as far as the eye could see. The taxi had dropped them on the bridge. It was chilly; March was only just pushing through out of winter and into spring, but it was enjoyable, and they found a quaint little Italian bistro to eat in.

"I am enjoying today," Cam said, taking another snap of Michelle as she gazed out over the balcony at a small boat passing by.

Michelle turned at Cam's voice and smiled. "Good! I'm glad," she said, reaching across the small table and taking her hand. She had felt a little guilty at forcing Cam to come here, especially now Cam had explained her family dynamic.

"I guess when you live somewhere you take it for granted. I have never looked at London from a tourist perspective before. It's a beautiful city."

"It is, and it gave me you, so I'm very grateful to it." Michelle grinned.

They ate and enjoyed each other's company, talking about the places they had been already and picking out some of the things they wanted to do over the coming days.

"I was thinking, while we're in town, maybe I should pop over to Art tonight and get it over and done with, then we can carry on just doing what we like for the rest of our stay."

"Is it not far then?"

"I wouldn't want to walk it," Cam laughed, "but a quick taxi ride will work."

"Okay, let's do it," Michelle replied. "But, remember, you promised hot and sweaty."

"Ah, so I did," Cam said, pulling her phone from her pocket and quickly calling Jo to arrange the meeting.

Chapter Thirteen

Music could be heard half a street away, but the loud din wasn't coming from Cam's bar. She was glad of that; otherwise she might have ended up in a battle with the locals about noise control. Instead, her bar was steadily filling up, and the music could be heard only when the door opened to allow anyone in.

They joined the end of the queue and waited in turn like everyone else.

"Why don't you just walk in?" Michelle asked as she wrapped her arms around Cam and snuggled up. It was more than chilly now as the night air dropped the temperature to something rarely felt in LA at this time of day. It could get cold in LA, especially at night during the winter months, but this was a different kind of cold. It seeped into your bones and stayed there.

Cam pulled her in closer, sharing her own body heat. She didn't mind the cold; years of living in it had made her somewhat immune. "Because I want to see how everyone works with the paying customer, and if we're giving the best service we can."

As they neared the end of the queue, Cam could see a tall, well-built black woman with long braids tied neatly at the back of her head. She was smart, dressed in pressed slacks, shirt, and tie as well as a navy jacket over it all, her security guard armband license on display around her upper left arm.

She looked the part and she acted the part. Cam was impressed. She could hear the chatter between her and the customers and it was good, friendly banter. She clearly knew some people better than others, but she was polite and courteous all around. *10/10 so far*, Cam thought.

When they got inside it was warm and welcoming; the only stares they got were appreciative ones from people admiring a good-looking pair of women. It was a busy night; a lot of people clearly enjoyed their time here, and laughter could be heard even above the music. The bar was made up of two areas. The upstairs part that was on ground level was mainly a bar and seating area, somewhere to pull up a chair and shoot the breeze with friends or with someone you hoped to get to know better before the evening was out. Downstairs was the dance floor and where the music could be heard coming from. Women continuously went back and forth from up to down and back again. No drinks were allowed downstairs unless they were in plastic glasses.

Cam pulled her jacket off, but Michelle kept hers on for now. The place was pretty packed, and Cam took her hand to lead her through the throng of female bodies that stood around talking, drinking, and watching. Couples hanging out with other couples. Single girls checking out the possibilities. Cam was reminded of a time not that long ago when she was just like these girls.

She pushed her way in and found a small gap at the bar. Leaning forward, she waved a twenty-pound note in the air to get someone's attention.

"What can I get ya?" a young, hip-looking girl with short spikey hair shouted across the bar at her. Cam thought she looked a lot like Erin probably had, fifteen years ago.

"Two bottles of Sol," Cam hollered back, handing over the twenty. When the young bartender returned with the drinks and change, Cam told her to keep it, earning her a huge smile in return.

She passed one of the bottles to Michelle and then turned to survey the room. It looked good. Pieces of art hung on the walls, exhibited for free for local artists trying to break into the business. She couldn't find fault with much at all, and she was pleased about that.

Finishing her drink, Cam waved over the same bartender. "Can you tell Jo that Cam Thomas is here to see her?" If the girl was shocked, then she hid it well, and Cam knew Jo had given the best behaviour speech. She leant in to Michelle and said, "I'll be back as soon as I can... be prepared to get all hot and sweaty with me."

Michelle laughed. "Oh, don't worry. I have plans for you, baby."

"You'll be okay? You can come with me if you want, I just figured it would be boring for you."

"Go, I'll be fine right here." She looked across the bar at the two girls working. They were whispering behind hands and seemed to be a little excited that Shelly Hamlin was at the bar. "I have a feeling I'm not going to be bored."

~Yes~

Once Cam had disappeared upstairs, Michelle settled back against the bar and looked around. She liked the place. It was exactly how Cam had described it: small, eclectic, and bijou, but it had something about it that she liked. The art on the walls was a fantastic idea and gave you something to enjoy or debate while you grabbed a drink after work by yourself or sat with a group of friends on a Saturday night.

As she glanced around, contemplating the idea of Camryn opening something similar in LA, she noticed a woman on the opposite side of the room staring over at her. She was used to it. People recognised her everywhere she went, and often they would be a little too nervous to directly speak to her, so they just stared. Michelle picked up her drink and took a swig. It was almost empty.

She smiled quickly at the woman, in a friendly but not interested way, and was surprised when the woman didn't return it. She turned her attention elsewhere and got the attention of the girl behind the bar and ordered another beer. She checked her phone for any messages while she waited. One from Robbie telling her to let Cam know that Zac made the soccer team and would be calling her for advice the minute they were back home. Quickly she replied that Cam would be teaching him that it was football, not soccer. The thought of Cam teaching Zac made her smile; they were best buddies. When they finally did have kids, she knew already that Camryn Thomas would be a wonderful mother.

When she looked up from her phone she noticed the same woman, still watching her, but she had moved a few seats closer. She looked tall, not as tall as Cam but getting there. She had long black hair and wore her jeans low over very slim hips. There was a sadness about her, something deep inside that made her face look like she was permanently frowning. She would have been attractive under other circumstances.

Michelle found herself searching for Gavin. She shook her head at how easily she had gotten used to having someone there to protect her. Not that this woman seemed to pose any threat, but she had never imagined that she would ever have had to deal with a Jessica in her life either, so she wasn't going to relax just yet.

It took a few more minutes before the woman finally plucked up the courage to move the last few feet. She licked her lips nervously and had her hands jammed into her jeans pockets. She fidgeted about from one foot to the other, and Michelle understood instantly that there was nothing to be worried about with her.

Finally, she spoke. "Hello, are you Shelly Hamlin?" She was polite enough in her inquiry, her voice quiet and educated.

"Uh yes, but I'd rather not shout that too loudly if you don't mind." She smiled. "I'm just here with my wife for business."

"I had hoped you would be," the mysterious woman continued.

Michelle worried a little more. Who was this woman, and what did she want with Cam? "I'm sorry, who are you exactly?"

"Oh, sorry. Kate, my name is Kate."

Chapter Fourteen

Cam came down the stairs laughing at something the older woman beside her had said. Jo wasn't anything like the person Michelle had imagined. She was short and stocky, wore a suit, not a dress like she had thought she would, and her hair was cut more like Gavin's than the blonde updo Michelle had in mind. She reminded herself not to assume.

The laughter stopped in an instant. The moment Cam laid eyes on the woman sitting nervously beside her wife at the bar, all mirth and merriment were replaced instantly with anger and nausea.

Kate had heard that old familiar laugh and readied herself for the reaction Cam would certainly have. When the blond head of her old friend came into view finally, she sucked in a breath, pushing the nauseous feeling down as their eyes met for the first time in over two years. They sized each other up, Cam like a coiled spring ready to attack, Kate looking more likely to run.

Michelle reached out to Cam and placed her palm against her bicep. She felt Cam tense the muscle there and then relax it as she registered who it was that was touching her.

"Babe?" Michelle hesitated. Maybe if this wasn't the best place to do this. "Kate wondered if she could have a quick chat with you," Michelle urged, knowing this wouldn't be an easy challenge to overcome.

"No," came the instant reply. She hadn't even thought about saying yes. She had nothing further to say. This woman had done something Cam had found unforgivable, and Michelle couldn't blame her for not wanting to speak to her.

"Cam? It might help to hear her out," Michelle tried again. She wouldn't push it, but she had a feeling it would do Cam good to hear her out, or at least, get some things off her chest.

Cam turned from Kate and faced Michelle, her blue eyes as cold as ice as she simply stated the obvious. "No."

Michelle nodded, smiling briefly. "Okay, then let's leave." The last thing Michelle wanted was for the situation to escalate. She had listened to Kate, heard the one side of the story that Cam hadn't. Nothing was as clear-cut as Camryn thought it was, and she hoped that if Cam could just find a way to listen, it might give her the answers she had needed.

"No, I am not leaving." Petulance now asserted itself. "We came here to have fun and dance. She..." She pointed at Kate. "Can do one."

Michelle pushed herself up close and personal with Cam. She reached up and wrapped her palm around the back of Cam's neck, tugging her forward so that her lips could speak as close to her ear as possible.

"I am going to say this just once, and you are going to listen to me. Then if you still say no, we are leaving, and I won't say another word about it, okay?" She stood back and waited for Cam to nod. Once she did, she leant back in and spoke again. "You need to listen to her and hear her side of things. It isn't as black and white as you think it is, as it appeared to be. Do you understand me?" She waited again for Cam to nod that she did. "So, do you want to listen, or leave?"

She pulled back again and looked Cam square in the eye. Cam knew one thing, and that was that she trusted Michelle with her life, her heart, and everything she had. She glanced over at Kate, who stood there looking like a lost puppy that had been kicked. She looked back at Michelle.

"Fine, 5 minutes," she said to Kate, who for the first time half-heartedly smiled. "Jo, can I use your office, please?"

~Yes~

Michelle directed Cam to sit in Jo's chair. She told Kate to take the seat opposite and then she pulled over a spare one and sat herself between them. From her position, she would act as referee if needed. She hoped that wouldn't be necessary, but with Cam puffing her chest and making herself the most dominant force in the room, and Kate looking as though she might die of fright on the spot, she was prepared. The three of them sat that way, silently, for what felt like an age, before finally, Cam spoke.

"Well, it's now 4 minutes. So, get it off your chest and let us all move on." She was hard-faced and angry. Rightfully so, she considered. The last thing she had expected was to see Kate right now. She wasn't prepared for it.

Kate nodded, understanding the animosity she was feeling from Camryn. She hadn't expected anything different. If anything, she had prepared herself for a slap, and she would have taken it, because really, she probably deserved it. "She told you that I was sexually attracted to her, right?" Her voice was not as timid as it had been earlier. This was her one chance, and she wasn't going to fuck it up. Not this time.

Cam nodded her assent to that question. Neither of them needed any reminding who *She* was.

"Okay, well I wasn't. It wasn't her I was attracted to..."

Cam grimaced. "I really don't care who you were attracted to, you fucked my girlfriend in my own bed, Kate!" Her voice was raised instantly, as was her anger. She had better things to be doing than listening to Kate talk about her love life. She glanced at her wife and silently questioned where this was going. She received her answer in a glare.

Kate nodded, her cheeks burning as she remembered back to that fateful day. "Yes, but not because I wanted to."

Cam rolled her eyes. "Seriously, I don't have time for this."

Michelle turned her glare back on Cam. "Let her explain, babe."

"Why?" Cam argued before turning back to Kate. "This is ridiculous, you weren't exactly tied down and forced."

Kate looked away, "No, I know how it looked. You're right, I wasn't physically forced." Shaking her head slowly and fidgeting on her chair, she tried to think of the best way to explain herself.

"Just spit it out Kate, you're down to 3 minutes now," Cam said, looking at her watch for dramatic effect. Michelle reached out, her fingertips resting lightly on Cam's forearm. Cam turned and looked at her. It was always calming; any time Cam got worked up, Michelle could calm her with just a touch.

"This isn't exactly easy to say, Cam." Kate's voice took on an air of anger itself as she finally blurted out what she needed to say.

"Well it wasn't exactly easy to witness, Kate," Cam spat back. Her fingertips squeezed and she relaxed back into her seat again.

It was then that Kate spoke again, her words tumbling out so fast that Cam wasn't sure she heard her correctly. "The truth is, I don't know...I don't know what happened because...one minute we were just talking, and then everything changed."

Cam stared at her, her eyebrows furrowed, eyes narrowing as she thought about those words. "Ya think?" She threw her hands up in the air and shook her head in disbelief that she was even listening to this.

Kate turned to Michelle for guidance. The actress nodded at her with a reassuring smile. "Just tell her, Kate."

Michelle's face said it would all be okay, if she just told Cam the truth. And for some reason, she trusted the American. Slowly, she turned back to face Cam. "I think she drugged me."

"What?"

"Everything was fine. We had some juice and were talking about ideas for the perfect gift...for you. She suggested something and laughed it off as a joke."

"What suggestion?"

Kate blushed. "She thought you'd want a threesome."

"With you?" She grimaced, not because Kate wasn't attractive, but the idea of her best friend in bed with her was just wrong, on every level.

Kate covered her face in her hands. Slowly, she pulled her palms down her face until just her mouth was covered by them. She sighed. "I thought she was joking too. I just laughed it off. I hadn't really noticed how closely she was sitting next to me," Kate all but whispered. There was no going back, not if she wanted to exorcise her own demons, give Cam the explanation that she deserved. "I started to feel strange...I've never felt like that before and then Jess...she started talking about you and her and things you did together, in bed. And it just felt, I dunno, sexy? Everything she said was sexual. It was like I had no control over my libido. I went from fine to horny in what felt like minutes, but I know now that it was longer than that."

Cam sat silently listening to her friend. If she believed her, then she didn't like where this was heading.

"I'm not like that Cam, you know me. You always used to laugh because I'd make them wait three dates before I even thought about sleeping with them. But with her, right then, it was all I could think about. It was like a switch had been turned on and..." She looked away, embarrassed. "I knew what I was doing was wrong, but...in that moment all I could think about was getting off, and the entire time she was there, whispering in my ear. Touching me..." She closed her eyes at the memory and tried not to get upset. It didn't help. Anytime she thought about it, it upset her. "I didn't want it to be her, Cam. I'd never have done that to you, but I couldn't...something was making me...it was like every inhibition I ever had just evaporated, and then she was kissing me and taking my clothes off and..."

Cam's thoughts were all over the place. She remembered the jokes at Kate's expense, how she did always make them wait. Then she remembered back to that day. When she had come home to find them in her bed. Only now she was remembering just how Kate had looked: glazed.

It took several seconds before Jessica threw her head sideways in the midst of her impending orgasm and opened her eyes. Like a startled rabbit, her senses refocused the instant she recognised Camryn standing there in the doorway. Her hand slowly lowered and pushed Kate away.

Kate's eyes rose from their concentrated glazed stare, a questioning frown on her face. It didn't take long for her brain to register the same startled gape as she looked straight into the pain-stricken, glowering eyes of her friend.

"Enough," Cam said sharply. "I don't need a re-run, I saw it," she spat. "I saw it...you and her." She shook her head. She too was stuck with the memory of that day. Had everything she assumed to have happened been something worse, something even more awful? She hadn't given Kate a chance to explain.

"Just get out, get out Kate." Cam was numb; her emotions had switched off. She couldn't afford to be emotional, to let them see what they had done, how they were destroying her. No, they wouldn't get to see that, to take that from her.

Kate turned to Jessica, silently pleading with her to do something, anything, but she just sat there avoiding eye contact. "Are you going to tell her?" Kate, her one-time best friend, screeched at her so-called lover.

Michelle had sat back listening to the exchange, but now she bent forward and added her own thoughts. "It sounds very much like Kate was drugged. I know of several actresses who have described similar experiences."

Cam looked at her wife and considered things, then she turned back to Kate. "Why didn't you tell me any of this?"

"I tried. You wouldn't hear me. I sent you emails, texts, you wouldn't take my calls. I even went back to the flat to talk to you, but all I found was Jessica. I confronted her of course."

"What did she say?" Cam's voice was softer now as she began to understand things better.

Kate smiled sadly at the memory. "She smirked at me and said I couldn't prove anything, and that it didn't matter now anyway because you had gone." She breathed deeply and exhaled before adding, "And then she asked if I wanted to do it again. That you coming home when you did, had meant that she had been left high and dry." She shuddered at the memory that was stirred. "I told her that she was crazy if she thought I'd go anywhere near her. That was when she said that a little Molly would soon loosen me up again."

Cam squinted at her in confusion.

"I discovered that Molly is slang for MDMA...from what I have read on it, I assume that was what she used." She shrugged. "But I can't prove any of this."

Cam fidgeted. She wasn't sure she wanted to know anymore. Kate's voice faded away. It was like a whole new can of worms just waiting to ruin her life again. Kate was still talking; she wanted to scream at her to shut up, and yet she couldn't, because deep down, she needed to know. She had to know the truth of it all, finally.

"Alright, let's say I believe this little story. Then that means..."

"She raped me," Kate answered for her as she stood up to leave. "I don't expect you to forgive me or to even want to speak to me again, but I wanted you to know the truth and the facts. So you could at least hate me for the right reasons."

There was a battle raging within Cam. She had been angry for so long, desperate to forget about them all, and then she had met Michelle and everything seemed to be going just great. But, Kate had been her best friend. Her one and only confidant. That was why it had hurt so much. And now it was hurting for a different reason. Because, if she was honest with herself, it had never added up. Kate was straight. Kate was honest and she was a bit of a prude. Finding her, of all people, in bed with Jessica had been unbelievable and yet, she had seen it with her own eyes. Or had she? Had her own hurt and pride stopped her from seeing what was obvious?

"Wait." She surprised herself as much as Kate.

Kate stood motionless at the door. She didn't dare turn around. She held her breath. Tears filled her eyes and threatened to spill over the second she dared to blink. Her mind was spinning as she silently prayed that Cam would give her a chance.

Cam stood up, still looking at her. "How did you know I would be here tonight?"

The question threw her, and it took a moment for Kate to find her words. "I read an article online about you that said you owned this and another bar in LA. I've been coming here once a week for the last 8 months hoping to find you here. Eventually I made friends with some of the staff, they look after the locals really well." She tried a smile, but it wasn't returned. "Someone called earlier and said you were coming tonight."

"We will be in London for a further 10 days," Cam said, more softly now. She reached into her pocket for a business card and held it out for Kate to take. "Maybe we can have dinner or something one night?"

"That would be really nice," Kate said. She risked a smile and this time, albeit thin-lipped and small, it was returned.

~Yes~

The cold air hit them both hard as they left the bar a lot earlier than they had originally anticipated. Michelle linked arms with Cam as they slowly ambled away from the bar towards traffic. People jostled past in the other direction. Cam kept one eye on the road in case a taxi appeared, but mainly her thoughts were on the night's events.

"Thank you," Cam said, leaning in to kiss the side of Michelle's head.

"You're welcome," she answered with a smile. "How do you feel about it?"

"Hmm not sure yet, like the biggest shit in the world?" Cam admitted. She glanced to her left at the woman who seemed to solve all the Jessica-related issues in her life.

"It's going to take some time."

Cam sighed. "I feel so selfish. Jessica ruined so much of my life, but what about Kate? How does she live with that?"

"I guess she has her own coping mechanisms and maybe she has had some therapy," Michelle reasoned.

"I wish she had told me, forced me to listen."

"Would you have believed her?" Michelle snuggled in closer. It was definitely colder now as they neared the river.

"I don't know, maybe not right away, I mean it's crazy, right? But I think in time I would have seen Jess for what she was."

"You were with her for over a year. If you hadn't walked in on them, maybe she would have continued to manipulate you."

"I guess so." Cam came to a stop outside of a souvenir shop. *I love London* t-shirts hung in the window. Display shelves were filled with miniature red buses and tiny red post-boxes. Paddington Bears and cuddly soft lions wearing England shirts lined the top shelf.

Michelle moved to stand in front of her, pressed up close to keep warm. "Maybe to a certain extent, you have to be thankful that things turned out the way they did. If you hadn't walked in on them?"

"I might still be with her," Cam finished for her, and then leant forward to press a kiss against Michelle's red nose. "And I'd never have met you, or won all this money, and I'd be totally oblivious to how happy I could have been instead," she said, her face lighting up as she said the words. She was happy, really happy.

"Exactly, and what Jessica did to Kate, she would still have done, you couldn't have known she had that planned. There wasn't anything you could do to prevent that."

"I know, doesn't stop it hurting."

"I know, but what happened is on Jessica, not you, Camryn." She wrapped her arms around Cam's neck and pulled her close. "It isn't your fault, okay?"

Cam nodded against her, nuzzling into her neck. She placed a warm kiss there.

"So, what can I do to help cheer you up?" Michelle grinned as she pulled back to look at her.

"Buy one of these shirts?" Cam laughed as she looked over Michelle's shoulder back to the shop front window. Michelle glanced backwards over her shoulder too.

"Uh no!" Michelle laughed along with her. "Come on, it's getting cold and we need to eat something. Let's go home."

"*Or* let's go in here and buy a hoodie to keep you warm and then find some little romantic restaurant where I can woo you."

"Cam! You don't need to woo me," she leant in to whisper. "Sex is a given."

"Aw, don't take all the fun out of it, babe." Cam winked and pulled her close. "Have I told you today how much I love you?"

Michelle shook her head, smiling.

"How remiss of me, I will have to buy you this hoodie to make amends and prove how much I love you." She laughed and dragged her into the shop to buy matching hoodies and t-shirts for everyone they knew!

Chapter Fifteen

Cam's childhood had been pretty good for the most part, and she planned to show Michelle around her old school. They drove south, away from the city and out to the suburbs and the small town that Cam had grown up in. She felt a little lighter in her step since talking with Kate and had a newfound energy about her as she weaved through the traffic with ease. She even sung along to some of the songs she recognised on the radio.

They started off a few miles from where Cam lived. The hospital where Cam was born was where she planned to start. It was just a quick drive by, nothing much to see now as most of it had been demolished and rebuilt on. There were brand new houses and a small block of flats that were still under construction.

Next on the magical history tour was Cam's first school. Perry Street Infants and Juniors was still there. Little kids ran around the playground screaming. Cam smiled at the sight. From the age of 3 until she was 11, she had been at this school, right through from nursery until she left to go to the secondary school her parents had picked for her. It all looked so much smaller as they walked past the fencing and looked in.

Bishopthorpe Secondary Modern was exactly how she remembered it. She drove slowly in through the gates and pulled the car into a marked space. Cam held Michelle's hand as they began wandering the grounds. They'd reached the old building, and Cam pointed at windows to the rooms Kate and herself had been educated in. It was a nostalgic day altogether, but as they reached the playground area and she was explaining how she and Kate had bunked off one afternoon and hidden out here, she froze.

"Camryn Thomas, stop right there," a rather loud and stern voice boomed from behind. Michelle looked around to see an older woman strolling towards them.

"Oh my God," said Cam, still frozen to the spot. "Is she coming?" She spoke out of the corner of her mouth, and Michelle couldn't suppress the giggle as Cam reverted back into the teenager she once was. She shoved her hands into her pockets and hunched her shoulders, shrinking several inches.

"The grey-haired lady?" Michelle asked, still smiling as she looked back and forth between them.

Cam nodded.

"Yes."

"Shit."

Michelle laughed again.

"Camryn Thomas, I thought it was you." The voice softened as the woman drew close.

Cam sucked in a deep breath and turned, ready to pull on the charm. She swung around with a huge smile on her face. "Mrs Hancock. How are you?"

"I am quite well, thank you, Camryn. I am surprised to see you here, after all you spent most of the last year you were meant to be here trying not to be so," she said a wry smile on her face.

"I do believe you are right, Mrs Hancock." She indicated Michelle. "Can I introduce you to my wife, Michelle?"

"Hello Mrs Hancock." Michelle smiled sweetly and reached out her hand to the older woman.

"Ah an American, lovely to meet you, dear," she said, reaching out to take the proffered hand. "How on earth have you ended up with this one?" She winked, smiling kindly and letting them both know she was just enjoying making Camryn squirm.

"Well, I don't think I had any choice in that." Michelle laughed and they both smiled at her candid answer. Nobody could ever deny the love that was written on both women's faces when they glanced at one another.

"So, what has brought you here today, Camryn?"

"Oh well, we are visiting London on our honeymoon, and Michelle wanted to see where I went to school."

"Oh, congratulations then. I think I read somewhere that you made a success of yourself. I am very pleased you met your potential eventually Camryn, I wasn't sure you would after dealing with some of your tricks."

Cam had the decency to blush, and she laughed nervously. The idea of Mrs Hancock regaling Michelle with every tale of mischief that she, usually along with Kate, had got up to in her teenage years, wasn't something she had envisaged at the start of the day.

"Well, yes I...okay, what do you want?" she said, smiling. "What do I have to buy the school to stop you telling all my secrets right now?"

They all chuckled as Michelle added, "Oh no, do tell, please."

"Come on Camryn, Michelle, let's go and see if we can find Mr Jones and Mrs Flynn. I would imagine they will be in the staff room by now, and I'm sure they would love to see you too."

They followed behind as the older woman led them into the school building. Cam felt like she was 14 again. The main part of the school was pretty much unchanged. The paint on the walls was a different colour, and some of the classrooms were different, but it was still very recognisable as the school she used to go to. She had had some good times here, despite getting up to all sorts of no good.

When they reached the staff room Cam was a little nervous; she never expected any of her old teachers to be here, let alone 3 of them. As Mrs Hancock opened the door and walked in, all heads turned their way, and two gasped.

"Camryn. Goodness, how lovely to see you." Mrs Flynn was the first to react and stood, easily crossing the room to greet her old student.

"Indeed, how wonderful," added Mr Jones as he placed the kettle back down on the counter. "It's so lovely to see past pupils return."

"Yes, it's kind of weird being back, but lovely to see you all," Cam said, genuinely surprised that she was so recognisable still to these people that she hadn't seen for twenty years.

The school bell rang, and one by one the teachers groaned and began to move, heading back out to their next classes. Hundreds of footsteps could be heard in the hall as kids ran back and forth to get to their next classes too.

Mrs Hancock took the opportunity to take the couple around the school before they headed off to finish their day. As they wandered around, the one thing Cam noticed was how shabby a lot of it looked, but that was nothing compared the old gym – the word *old* being the most important. It looked like it hadn't been updated since Cam was there.

"Mrs Hancock?" Cam probed. "When was the last time the gym here was updated?"

She looked around and frowned. "It has been a while, Mrs Thomas." She smiled. Budgets were generally used to fulfil other parts of the curriculum; physical exercise always came last, along with the arts.

"It's Camryn, Mrs Hancock."

"It's Daphne, Camryn," she laughed.

"Oh man I can't call you Daphne, you're Mrs Hancock," Cam laughed.

"Of course you can, you haven't been in school for nearly 20 years. You're a young woman now, not a gobby teenager." Daphne Hancock smirked back at her. She hadn't changed much; even in Cam's days at the school she had had grey hair. Cam had liked her; she was a stern, but fair teacher. You didn't mess about in her class unless you were prepared for the consequences. Of course, Cam and Kate had pushed her limits on several occasions, but never to the point of getting into any real trouble.

"Ok, no need to rub that in." Cam laughed before becoming serious. "I want to build you a new gym."

"Camryn, I didn't take you on this tour so that you would do that."

Cam held up her palm to stop her. "I know you didn't. I still want to do it though. I can afford it, and it would be really nice to put something back."

"Well, I can't say that the current crop of children wouldn't appreciate it."

"Great, then I will leave my details with you and we can organise that."

Chapter Sixteen

When Kate Morris had received the call from Libby the previous day, telling her that Cam was in town and expected to arrive at the bar that evening, her nerves had almost gotten the better of her. She had gotten to the bar early and had a couple of beers to build some Dutch courage. When Cam had first walked in through the door, she thought she might actually throw up; she was that anxious. Instead, she melted away into the background and waited for her moment. Cam had left to join the manager upstairs, leaving Shelly Hamlin alone at the bar. She had taken the opportunity, the idea being that if she got short thrift from the actress, then she could leave knowing full well Cam would never listen, and she didn't want to hear Cam tell her to get lost. Michelle had clearly been a little worried at first, and Kate thought she would just get up and walk upstairs. She couldn't blame her if she had; she had read in the papers what Jessica had been up to in the States. That was another part of the reason she wanted to see Camryn, just to make sure she was alright. But Shelly hadn't walked away; instead she had listened. When she offered to help, Kate almost fainted.

Losing Camryn from her life had been devastating, but if she could remedy that now, then she was going to do all she could.

She had never had any real interest in women; her friendship with Cam had lasted over 20 years, and she had never considered her as anything other than her friend. But, the idea of sleeping with a woman had crossed her mind a few times. It was more like one of those fantasies that people had with no intention of ever really acting on it. Even now, she would remember back and shudder as memories flittered back.

Jessica pressed her thigh up against her. Leaning in, Kate could feel the swell of her breast against her arm as she reached across and turned a page in the gadgets catalogue they were looking through. She felt her skin heat. Her head was spinning with arousal that didn't make any sense to her, and yet, it was there.

"Maybe I should get Cam a new vibrator?" Jessica whispered, and then laughed. When did Jessica get such a sexy laugh, *Kate thought to herself. "Or something more exciting. God, she makes me so hot when she is making me..." Jess laughed and leant in even closer until her mouth was as close to Kate's ear as she could get. "Come." She moaned and let her tongue dart out to lick the edge of Kate's ear.*

"What are you doing?" Kate said, half-groaning at the feelings her body was experiencing. She felt light-headed, euphoric even, and nothing made any sense. This was Jessica, Cam's girlfriend, and yet....

"Do you feel good, Kate?"

"Yes...I mean, I don't know...God, I am hot."

"You are, I've always found you attractive," Jessica continued, much to Kate's confusion.

"No, I mean..." She fanned herself with her hand. "I'm hot, why is it so hot in here? Are you not..."

"I guess it is warm. Why don't you take some of those clothes off?" Jessica's hand was skimming lightly over Kate's thigh. She wanted to protest, but it just felt so, so good. She felt good, she felt happy, and so fucking aroused. Jessica's palm was now creeping up her abdomen, under her shirt. Her head was screaming at her to stop this, but her body was winning the battle. Her nerve endings were on fire as the delicate palm cupped her breast. Everything felt intensified. Her nipple hardened and strained to be released from its prison.

Kate lifted her top and was confused by the sound of Jessica whooping with excitement. "Shall I help you?" Jess asked. Without waiting for a reply, she reached for the button to Kate's jeans and popped it. The zip followed. She wanted to yank them off. They were too constrictive. She needed to be released from the confines of her clothes. Instead, she found herself soaring in pleasure when Jessica pushed her hand inside her underwear and rubbed her intimately.

"This is wrong," she whimpered against Jessica's lips, but she couldn't fight the intrusion of her tongue. She welcomed it and felt herself move against the talented fingers that were now inside her.

"Its not wrong, just go with it. You like it, don't you?" Jessica had said as she pulled back to watch her. "I wanna watch you come and then," she leant back in to her ear, sucking a lobe as her fingers sped up, "I want you to go down on me. I want to taste myself on your lips."

Kate shuddered now at the memory. She had tried hard to forget it. But it wasn't that simple. At night when she was alone, it infiltrated her dreams. She felt nauseous just thinking about the things she had done.

So, she had taken the bull by the horns and figured she had nothing to lose by going to Art and trying to speak to Cam. She knew she risked a slap, a public slanging match, or just being completely humiliated, but she had to try.

And now when she had a phone number and an invitation to call Cam, she was even more nervous, because Cam now knew, she knew what Jessica had done. And much to her delight, it seemed as though she believed her. It had been a difficult couple of years, but she was moving forwards, dating Michael, and though life wasn't perfect, it was better than it had been after Cam had left.

She didn't want to waste any more time though, so she gave herself a pep talk and punched in the number that Cam had given her. The phone rang four times before Cam answered.

"Hello." She was out of breath as she spoke, her voice light and happy. That thought made Kate smile. Knowing she was indeed happy meant everything to her.

"Hey, it's Kate." She could hear giggling in the background, and that made her smile even more. Cam was having fun, and happy!

"Hey, sorry hold on a sec," Cam said before she muffled the phone handset, but Kate could clearly hear her laughing and telling Michelle to go and get dressed. "Hi, sorry, so, hi," Cam said, not quite knowing what to say. It had been so long. Kate was someone she had spoken to at least once a day, every day, and yet now, she didn't know where to start.

"So, this is kind of awkward, right?" A nervous chuckle slipped out.

"Yes, it feels strange to be hearing your voice again," Cam admitted, but she was quietly elated that her old friend had called so soon. She had missed her, and if they could just get past this and find a way back to anywhere near who they were previously, then she wanted that.

"I was wondering when you would be free, to have dinner maybe?" Kate asked, getting to the point rather than dragging it out.

Cam agreed quickly. "Yeah, okay, that's sounds like a good idea."

"Okay, tomorrow? Did you want to go somewhere in particular, or I could come to you or vice versa," Kate offered, realising that she was beginning to ramble a little.

"Maybe we could go to that restaurant on Jermain St?"

"It closed about a year ago, but there is a nice place around the corner from there. It's called Lemon, it's Italian."

"Okay, Italian works for me." She switched the phone from one hand to the other as Michelle sidled up next to her and leant in. "I'll see you there at 7 then?"

"Great, I'll book us a table," Kate confirmed, before quickly asking, "Is Michelle coming?"

"Nope, just me I think unless, you know, you wanted to bring someone?"

"No, just us is fine, I'm looking forward to it," Kate said. She blew out the quiet breath she had been holding and smiled to herself. The first steps were always the hardest, and she was taking them.

"Yeah, me too," Cam replied. "Bye." She hung up and blew out a deep breath too.

"Was that Kate?" Michelle asked, stroking her palm along Cam's leg.

"Yes, we're having dinner tomorrow night. By ourselves, I hope that's okay with you?" She glanced down at the hand that was soothing her and placed her own on top of it, linking their fingers.

"Yes of course, I can find something to do with myself for an evening." She smiled, glad that Cam was trying to find a connection again with Kate. Even if all they did was clear the air and parted on good terms, it was better karma all around, but she had a feeling that once Camryn let her guard down a little, she would let Kate make amends.

"Why are you still in pyjamas?" Cam asked as she started to climb on top of her and tickle her sides. "You were supposed to be getting dressed to go out."

"Mm I thought about it, but I'd much rather stay in bed with you," she said, rising up to kiss her.

Chapter Seventeen

The restaurant was quaint and bijou, typical Kate really; she liked cosy and atmospheric rather than bold and outlandish. It was nice to think maybe she hadn't changed too much, Cam thought as she entered the restaurant. She had arrived early and was surprised to find Kate already there. A waitress greeted her and led her through to the table Kate was sitting at. She looked as nervous as Cam felt.

Cam waggled her fingers and smiled awkwardly as they approached and Kate caught sight of her. She stood as the waitress pulled out a chair for Cam. She looked nice, Cam thought. Her long dark hair flowed halfway down her back, and she smiled like she really meant it.

There was an awkward moment of not quite knowing what to do – hug? Shake hands? Just sit down? In the end they went for a brief hug and a kiss to the cheek, and that seemed to take the edge off of the nerves on both sides before Cam took her seat, smiling at the waitress in thanks.

"Can I get either of you a drink?" she asked, handing out menus to them both. Cam noticed the name tag on the girl's uniform: Carol.

"God yes," Cam smiled. "Vodka, lime, and soda please, Carol." She spoke with confidence and earned a bright smile for using the woman's name. How many people ate here and didn't even notice her?

"Can you make that two, please?" Kate added, quickly holding two fingers up to indicate that she too would have the same. They both watched silently as Carol smiled and turned, walking away from them towards the small bar in the corner. Cam was shaken from her thoughts when Kate began speaking. "I am truly sorry for everything I did, Camryn." She tentatively reached across the table for Cam's hand. "And I am so grateful to you for giving me this opportunity to..."

Cam interrupted her apology. "Kate, I think that we have both been the victim of a very calculated and callous person. We have lost enough time because of her. I'm not sure you should be apologising, but I hope you will accept mine?"

Kate looked confused, her brow furrowing as she looked across the table. "What on earth have you got to apologise to me for?"

Cam released her hand and sat back in her chair. Carol appeared and placed both drinks down on the table with a smile, looking at them expectantly. They hadn't even picked up their menus, so she backed away to give them a further minute or two. Cam took a sip of her drink and looked into her friend's eyes, eyes that once upon a time had been alive and smiling, but now looked as though they had been through a lifetime of sadness. "We were friends for 20-odd years and I never gave you the chance to explain, I just cut you off."

"You had every right to, Jesus," Kate cut in.

Cam raised her palm. "No, I was with her for 18 months and I gave her the chance to explain, I should have given you the same opportunity, and maybe all of this would have been avoided." They both remained silent. Cam picked up the menu and browsed before she placed it down again and looked back at Kate. "I just wish you had been able to tell me."

"Would you have believed me if I had?" Kate came back at her.

"I don't know. Michelle asked me the same thing. I'd like to think I would have, even if I didn't want to hear it."

"Maybe, I just..." Kate stared up at the ceiling as she considered her words. "I'm...when it happened I didn't really understand, ya know? I got outside and the cold air hit me, it was like I'd been drunk and suddenly I was sober and the last few hours were all a blur."

Cam sat forward and rested an elbow on the table, her chin in her palm, listening intently.

"I went home and I suddenly I was low, like really depressed low, and I figured it was because of what happened, because I was upset that you had... ya know, but it wasn't that. It was chemical. It felt like I'd had this huge high and now bam, I'd hit the other side. I slept for hours and then when I woke up, I kept getting these flashbacks. It all felt like some really surreal dream, but..." She blushed as she considered how to explain further. "I knew it was real, I knew it wasn't a dream because, I could feel that

I'd..." She grimaced at the memory. "I knew I'd had sex, and I had a love bite on my collarbone."

"Kate, you don't need to explain."

"I do, I need for you to know, to really know that I'd never, ever do that to you consciously."

"I know that now. I know now that Jessica used you, like she uses everyone, but I have to take my share of the blame. No matter what I thought I saw, I should have got the answers, I should have been there for you," Cam admitted, a wave of guilt washing over her as she acknowledged letting her friend down.

"You didn't know, so don't feel guilty." Kate spoke honestly, looking Cam in the eye as she said it. Carol reappeared, pad in hand, and looked at them both expectantly. They each quickly glanced at the menu and gave their order. Kate waited until she was gone before she spoke again, wanting to change the subject. "I read about what she did to you. I just couldn't believe it. Are you okay now?"

Cam shrugged. "Yeah, physically I am pretty good. I still have some physio now and then. It's a lot harder at the gym." She smiled. "I struggle with my scars, I never envisaged life with so many reminders of something so horrific."

"I can't even begin to imagine, it must have been just terrifying."

"It wasn't fun, especially the second time around."

"I feel so bad that I didn't speak up before about her," Kate said, her voice full of remorse and regret. "Maybe if I had..."

"Michelle pointed out something very important to me." Cam smiled. "If I hadn't come home when I did, I would most likely still be with her and I would never have known the love of my life or found myself in the position I am today to be able to do anything I want to."

Kate noted that Cam's face lit up whenever she mentioned Michelle. Having seen them together, she could see just how much Michelle understood Camryn, how she complemented her, and how very much she adored her.

Carol returned again, this time carrying two bowls of pasta. She placed one in front of each of them. They smiled and thanked her. When she moved away this time, Kate added, "I am glad you found Michelle, she seems like a perfect match for you."

"Ya know, sometimes I wake up in the middle of the night and have to turn over just to check she is really there." Cam blushed at her own admission as she stuck her fork into the spaghetti and twisted it.

"A movie star, Cam! You married a movie star!" Kate laughed.

"Yeah, I did. Crazy, right?"

Kate nodded. "You're not wrong."

The conversation seemed to flow more easily as the evening progressed. Kate told Cam all about Michael and how they had met at work. He was a nice guy, but she didn't think he was *the one.* But she was happy to have him for now.

Cam told Kate all about her club in LA, and they spent a good few minutes laughing about Mrs Hancock.

"I couldn't believe it when I heard her shout my name." Cam laughed.

Kate chuckled and shook her head. "She always did catch us."

"So, what are you doing now? Last time we spoke you was doing your teacher training course."

"Yeah, I did. I work in a school as a PE teacher."

"Enjoy it?"

Kate placed her fork down, finished with the meal. "It has its moments, but I am not sure I am cut out for teaching teenagers to keep fit." She smiled, but it didn't fool Cam. There was definitely more to Kate's life that she needed to catch up on.

Cam had enjoyed the evening so far. It was fun catching up with the woman that, before Michelle, had known everything there was to know about her, if not more. She decided to take a chance. "Would you like to come back to the flat and have a drink? I know Michelle would love to see you again and get to know you better."

Kate tilted her head at the offer. "Yeah, I think I would like that."

There was a brief argument over who would pay the bill. Cam won that battle, promising Kate that she could pay next time. There being a next time was the only reason Kate backed down. She didn't know when the next time would be, but Cam had said there would be one, so she acquiesced and smiled happily to herself, accepting the small victory.

Cam's car weaved through the traffic with ease as Kate followed behind in her own vehicle. She followed the hire car as it swung left and right on its way towards the river, before it disappeared into the underground parking. Cam parked and pointed to the spot alongside her marked visitor parking.

Coming out of the elevator, they were laughing about a time when Kate had had to defend Cam's honour when her trousers lost a button and fell down around her ankles in the playground. "Oh my God, I forgot all about that," Cam was saying as they walked through the door to her apartment. Kate passed her and walked into the hall as Cam turned and locked the door behind them.

"Wow Cam, this is a really great place!" Kate exclaimed as she caught a glimpse of the views across town out of the first window they passed.

"Yeah, it's got great views," she answered before turning back to the hallway and calling out to Michelle. "Hey honey, I'm home," she said with a giggle.

Kate followed her down the hallway and into the living area to find Michelle sitting and talking...to Cam's mother.

Chapter Eighteen

"Are you kidding me?" Cam said as she took in the sight of her mother comfortably sitting in her living room, drinking tea as though she had always belonged here. Cam studied her. She was a little greyer around the ears. Her hair was shorter than Cam remembered it. She had a few lines around the eyes, most people would call them laughter lines, but Cam didn't think there had been much laughter over the years since she had been an adult. But other than that, her mother looked well, and somewhere in the recess of her mind, she was intrigued as to why she was here.

Michelle stood quickly and crossed the room, eager to put an end to any possible argument. She seemed to be playing referee quite a lot lately. "Cam honey, uh, your mother is here," she said, stating the obvious and receiving a raised eyebrow from Camryn in response.

Cam considered things for a moment before she directed her attention past her wife and back to the woman who sat perched on the couch with a half-smile on her face. "What do you want?" She loved her mother, but she didn't like her very much right now. There was a lot of water under the bridge and right now she wasn't quite so sure she was able to deal with it.

Pippa Thomas visibly stiffened, the smile dropped from her face, and she drew in a deep breath. Michelle felt Cam tense as they waited for her mother to reply.

"Hello Mrs Thomas," Kate interjected as she looked around Cam, smiling and waving at the woman whose house she had virtually lived in as a teenager. Cam glared at her and mouthed the word traitor, before she smirked and Kate took a step back.

"Camryn, Katherine," her mother finally acknowledged, ignoring the original question. "Have you had a nice time?"

Nobody said a word. All eyes were on Camryn as they waited for her reaction.

"Mother, why are you?" she repeated before shaking her head. "Actually no, how did you even know I would be here?" Cam asked. She turned slowly and eyed Kate suspiciously.

Kate held her palms up. "I didn't say anything, I haven't seen your mum since you left."

Cam squinted at her but accepted her answer for now. She returned her glare back on her mother and waited again, determined to get an answer.

Michelle leant in and spoke quietly. "Be calm, sweetheart." She squeezed Cam's arm before catching Kate's eye and jutting her chin at the kitchen. Kate was quick to cotton on and followed her swiftly out of the room.

Cam bit her lip but nodded again, this time to herself. Michelle was right, she needed to keep calm. Breathing deeply, she settled herself and used some of the techniques she had learned these past months through her therapy sessions. The urge to lash out had been her first thought, but that wouldn't help, or be constructive. Reconciliation with Kate had taught her that finding answers made her feel better. And she needed answers from her mother right now too.

"Camryn, I... well if you must know, I looked on your Facebook page." Cam was impressed her mother even knew what Facebook was, let alone how to use it. However, it still didn't explain why she was here. "Your page had photos of you... \you and Michelle in Trafalgar Square. So, I took a chance in assuming you might still be in London and as I had your address from the last time you were here-"

"When you ignored me?" Cam interrupted. She was still yet to sit down, so she paced the room instead. A sudden urge to just flee came over her and she eyed the door. Just twenty feet and she could be out and away from all this. But her mother was speaking again, and she found herself drawn in to listen to her.

"From your last visit when I was unable to get away and visit you," her mother explained indignantly. Her eyes cut to the floor though, unable to hold eye contact with her daughter any longer. Those blue eyes, so alike her own, bore into her.

Cam felt a pang of guilt that she had made her mother feel bad. But she couldn't help how she felt; she had every right to be angry. Her mother had made absolutely no effort to contact her for years. "I see, and you can get away this time because?"

Pippa folded her hands in her lap and shifted a little before answering. She held her head high and turned to face her daughter before she finally stated, "I left your father."

It wasn't often Cam found herself doing a double take, but this was going to be one of those times. She looked up at her mother once more. "I'm sorry, what did you just say?" Their eyes locked and this time they held, until finally Cam looked away at the sound of Michelle and Kate returned with mugs of tea. There was a new tension in the room. They glanced at one another before returning their attention to both women. Cam was wide-eyed and silent. Her mother was trying to hold it together.

Michelle and Kate silently placed the mugs they were carrying onto the coffee table that stood between them all. Unsure what to do next, they both took a seat on the couch and waited it out.

Finally, Cam's mother repeated what she had said a moment ago. "I have left your father. I have told him that I want a divorce."

Stunned silence.

"And I am staying in Caroline's flat until she returns next month. Then I'll have to find somewhere of my own," she stated rather matter-of-factly, as though she had just announced what a lovely day it was.

Cam flopped down on the couch opposite her mother and just stared at her. Her mother had never once stood up to her father; she had always been the dutiful wife that did as she was expected, and yet, here she was telling her that she had not only left him but told him she wanted a divorce too.

Pippa continued when Cam didn't reply. "I wanted to see you before you went back. I have always wanted to see you, and I am ashamed to say I didn't fight hard enough for you when I should have." Her mother's tough exterior now melted away. Tears sprang to her eyes and Cam was unable to ignore it any longer. She got up and rushed to her mother's side, tentatively placing her arms around her shoulders. All the pain of missing her mum slipped away in an instant as she felt her those familiar arms wrap around her too.

"It's okay Mum, it's okay."

"I'm so sorry Camryn, I'm so sorry," she sobbed against Cam's shoulder. Michelle reached for Kate's hand and gripped it as both of them watched the scene play out in front of them.

"Mum, don't cry, he isn't worth it."

Pippa looked up and into eyes that had softened. "But, you are, and I let you down. I've missed so much."

"It's okay, you had to live with Dad, I didn't." Cam wanted to be understanding, to move forward. If this last year had taught her anything, it was that life was far too short, and once those walls had begun to crumble, she gave up trying to rebuild them. First Michelle had broken through, then Kate, and now she was looking at her mother and trying to remember why they had lost so much time together.

They sat talking quietly, catching up and connecting again. For Cam it was somewhat unreal; she had come back to England against her wishes, and only because she couldn't say no when her wife was asking in that way that made her heart beat faster and her head stop working. She looked around the living room at the woman that loved her, her ex-best friend, and now her mother, and she was glad of it all.

~Yes~

Cam yawned and out of habit, glanced at the clock. It was almost one a.m. "God, did you see the time?"

"Oh, wow, it is late, I should get going," Kate replied, rising to leave.

"We have a spare room, Kate, if you would prefer not to drive so late. You have had a couple of drinks," Michelle suggested, hoping Kate would take her up on the offer and extend the opportunity for her and Cam to talk some more in the morning.

"Are you sure? I wouldn't want to put you out."

"Of course Kate, it makes sense, and you too Mum, we have enough room. You should stay, both of you," Cam insisted.

~Yes~

Michelle lay cradled in the crook of Cam's left arm. Her own left arm was slung casually across Cam's middle, lightly stroking up and down her ribcage, her fingers occasionally skimming over a scar. Cam's breath hitched, and she wiggled as Michelle found a ticklish spot.

"You okay, sweetheart?" Michelle asked, leaning up on her elbow to look down on Cam.

"Yeah, just kind of mind-fucked." She laughed. "This is all your fault, ya know?"

"Me?" Michelle laughed lightly, her fingers walking up the centre of Cam's abdomen.

"Yes, you. You wanted to come here. I wanted an island ,remember?" She pulled her closer, trapping her hand between them as it covered her breast.

"Oh, yeah I do remember you mentioning that," Michelle chuckled, pressing a kiss against the skin in front of her.

"Thank you," Cam said, returning the kiss to the top of Michelle's head.

"Go to sleep baby, you have guests to attend to in the morning." Michelle laughed again, lifting her head to gently place a kiss on Cam's chin. "I will be sleeping in." The grin on her face was all Cam needed to see in order to sleep peacefully.

Chapter Nineteen

Still lying nestled warmly against her wife, Michelle was increasingly aware of Cam's light snore. She giggled to herself. Cam's features looked more relaxed and at peace than she had ever seen them. The morning had brought with it a harmony that had settled. She could already tell that Cam would feel lighter.

It was still early, and the apartment was silent. Nobody else was up yet, and she took a moment to just enjoy the silence.

She caught the sunlight bouncing off her wedding ring and brought her hand closer to her face to look at it. In moments like this she often had the feeling of needing to pinch herself. She was married, to a woman no less. And not just any woman, but Camryn Thomas, the love of her life and the hereafter.

They had been through so much together already, and yet it had been less than a year still. Lesser couples would never have made it through, but they had, and they were stronger for it. They had always had a connection, something innate that drew them together, but the bond they shared from the turmoil with Jessica was something that had grown exponentially by itself, and she relished it. Now, as she watched bridges build and painful wounds heal, she was aware of a new aspect of their life that would extend and hold them together: family, Cam's family.

She slipped gently from Cam's embrace and the bed to creep to the kitchen, making a cup of coffee that she took back to their room. She placed the cup on the bedside table to cool a little, and then she headed to the bathroom for a quick shower.

Clad in just a towel, Michelle sat back down on the edge of the bed and picked up her mug, the coffee now at a drinkable temperature. She thought back to the previous night when Cam had gone out to try and find some way of salvaging her friendship with Kate. The last thing she had expected was Cam's mother turning up. She had imagined that her first meeting with the woman might have entailed giving her a piece of her mind, but once she had answered the intercom and invited her up, she was more intrigued than anything.

"Hello, you must be Shelly?" She sounded just like Camryn. Standing on the other side of the door with her coat on and a bag slung over her shoulder, she looked uncomfortable, fidgeting just the same as Cam did when she was anxious.

It crossed Michelle's mind now that she knew very little about the woman that had birthed and raised her wife. "Yes, and...I'm sorry, I don't know your name."

"Phillipa, but Pippa will do." Her smile was a little unsure and nervous. "I was hoping to speak with Camryn, is she...?"

"Cam's out right now," Michelle interjected before she stepped to one side and held the door open. "Please, come in and wait, she won't be long."

Crossing the threshold, Pippa said, "Thanks, if you're sure?"

Michelle wasn't sure as she closed the door, and she wondered if this really was the right thing to do. Cam was not going to be expecting this when she walked through the door later. "Of course, may I take your coat?" She tried to smile as Pippa shrugged off the heavy jacket, but she only managed a thin-lipped grin. Regardless of the fact that she was clearly Cam's mother, Michelle was not impressed.

Pippa Thomas waited until Michelle turned and walked back towards the kitchen. "Would you like a drink? Tea? Coffee? Something stronger?" she offered, indicating the living room where Pippa Thomas could sit. "Please, make yourself at home."

"Thank you, a cup of tea would be lovely."

She made a pot of tea and brought it, along with china cups and saucers, a milk jug and sugar bowl, into the living room on a tray. It all looked so quaint. They sat in silence while she poured two cups and Michelle considered once more how it was that a woman could completely ignore her child.

"Why are you here?" Michelle blurted. She hadn't intended to, but the words had just slipped out. Anger bubbled beneath the surface.

Pippa sighed, accepting that it was a valid question, even if it was one she had hoped to avoid. "You could say that I have finally come to my senses." When Michelle failed to speak, she continued. "I have a lot to make up for, I know that."

Michelle stared at her, studied her a little. She could see the resemblance. Something about the eyes were familiar to her. "I called Caroline," Michelle finally said, "When Camryn was..." She still found it hard to say. "When we didn't know if she would live, I called her and hoped she would call you."

The cup Pippa held in her hand stopped just short of her lips and she placed it back down on its saucer. "I didn't know. Caroline is not at home very much; her work takes her to places where she can't always call. By the time we found out...well, I didn't think I'd be welcome." Now, it was her turn to study her daughter-in-law. She was so confident in the way she held herself. "I've never been a brave woman. It always seemed so much easier to just bury my head in the sand..." Her voice trailed off as the lump in her throat grew larger. "Do you think...she will want to see me?"

Michelle considered the question for a moment. "Knowing Cam? Yes, I think she will...but, I won't let you hurt her again." Michelle spoke with confidence. "She has been through so much this past year already. So, if you're here for any other reason than working things out, starting with an apology, then you need to leave now."

The sunshine hadn't lasted very long. Dark clouds had blown in fast and angry. Rain lashed down, hitting the windows with a frantic tap, tap, tap. The wind was loud this high up, and Cam stirred. A sleepy smile graced her face as her eyes flickered open. She squinted at the light and blinked a few times as her eyes adjusted to wakefulness.

Relief swept over Michelle as she understood by just looking at her that Cam was going to be just fine.

"Morning," Michelle whispered, leaning down intent on claiming a kiss. Cam turned her mouth away and grinned.

"Hold that thought. Morning breath," she exclaimed, jumping from under the covers and running naked into the bathroom. When she returned, Michelle was dressed. "Aw, spoilsport." She grinned, spinning Michelle around to face her. "I wasn't that long," she said, her words meeting lips that pressed against her own.

"Mm, minty fresh."

~Yes~

The kitchen, for such a big place, was rather small and sparse in Michelle's opinion. Not that she minded right now as Cam pushed her back against the closest countertop and kissed her with an intensity that she usually saved for moments when they could follow it up. Hands grabbed at her hips and she let her own palms slide easily over Cam's shoulders, fingers pushing into her hair and pulling her closer. The sound of someone coughing gently brought them to an end. Michelle bit her lip and tried not to blush as Cam's mother stood in the doorway watching them.

Cam let her head rest against Michelle's forehead a second before she turned to face her mother.

"Sleep well, Ma?" Cam asked with a smile as she watched Michelle leave the room. Another minute and her mother might have interrupted a lot more than a kiss. Cam smirked at the idea as she lifted the kettle and began to pour hot water into cups.

"Sorry, I didn't mean to...Yes, thank you Camryn, I slept very well, thank you."

Cam smiled at her. "Great, so I was going to talk to you about something." She added a little milk and passed a mug across to her mother, before doing the same for herself.

"Okay."

"So, the thing is... why don't you come back to the States with us?" She leant back against the countertop, chewing her lip. Had she just asked her mother to come and live with them?

"To America?"

"Yeah, it's my home now and...well, you could come and stay for a while and we could...we could keep talking." She smiled shyly and hoped.

"Oh, you're not going to stay here then?" Her mother seemed disappointed at that.

Cam's smile dropped. "No, why would I? My life is in LA. Michelle, my friends, our family and my business, plus with Michelle's career..."

"Of course, I didn't think." She half smiled at Cam, considering her options. "Okay, I think that would be nice."

Chapter Twenty

As quickly as the storm had rolled in, the wind dropped, the rain stopped, and the sun was back out and shining through the clouds. Spring in England. Michelle thought that it pretty much summed up Cam's life lately.

Cam was wasting no time ensuring her mother really did come back with them, for however long she wanted to stay. Cam would take whatever was on offer for now. She hoped her mother would stay long enough, but if she wanted to return then Cam would make sure she was okay. She could stay here if she wanted to, in the apartment.

"Do you need me to come and help you pack, Mum?" Cam asked, sitting down on the arm of the couch.

Kate had already left an hour earlier as she had a job to go to and couldn't take any time off, even though she wanted to. It had been great to spend as much time together as they had, and they had said goodbye with hugs and a few tears and of course the promise to visit soon. Both of them were grateful for the second chance.

"No Camryn, but I will call you when I am done, and you can come and pick me up if that's okay?" her mum said as she rifled through her handbag for keys.

"Yeah sure. I just worry." She was chewing her lip again, filled with a nervous apprehension.

"He won't be any trouble, Camryn. He might be a stubborn, close-minded old misery guts, but he has never laid a hand on me, and if he starts today then he will come off worse, I can assure you," she said, reaching back into her bag and pulling out a small canister of pepper spray.

"Where the heck did you get that?" Cam laughed.

"Apparently your sister was worried too, this arrived by courier a few days ago."

Cam continued to laugh. Things really had changed while she had been away.

"Okay, so you will call me when you're ready then?"

"Yes, now stop worrying and go and enjoy the rest of the day with your wife." Pippa kissed her daughter on the cheek and gently squeezed her arm. "I'll be fine, Camryn."

"Alright, look Mum, this is my number now." She held out a card and Pippa took it. She looked at it and entered Cam's new number into phone, and then she called Cam's phone.

Cam read the display, the smile on her face widening as she added to contacts and typed in "Mum."

~Yes~

They pulled up outside the house that Cam had called home for her entire childhood. It wasn't much, just a semi-detached with adjoining garage and a tiny front yard. She looked up at the top window, her old bedroom, and for a moment she felt a pang of regret, mixed with belonging. There had been a lot of laughter and love inside those walls once.

"You can come in if you like," Pippa said from her seat in the back of the car.

"Maybe another time, eh Mum?" she said, glancing up at her mother through the rear-view mirror.

"Of course, you two go and enjoy yourselves and I'll call you when I am ready." She opened the door and climbed out. Cam pressed the button that would bring her window down and leaned out.

"Mum, can you bring some old photos with you?" Pippa smiled and nodded. She turned then and made her way up the path. Cam watched until she had the key in the door and it opened. Once she was safely inside, Cam put the car into gear and pulled out into the road.

"She will be fine," Michelle offered, her fingers gripping Cam's thigh gently. Cam turned her attention back to the road and sighed.

"I know." She nodded to herself before chancing a quick glance to her left. "It's just weird, I never thought I'd be here again, ya know?"

"I imagine that it would be. You grew up here, it has a lot of memories for you."

"It did." Cam settled back into her chair and looked ahead at the traffic as the car came to a halt. "He's probably at home," she announced suddenly, referencing her father.

"Do you wanna go back? Talk to him?"

Cam shook her head vehemently. "No. I don't even know what I would say to him anymore." She bit her lip and thought about it; she definitely wasn't ready to talk to him right now. "It just hurts. He's my dad and he should..." She swallowed the lump down.

"He should love you for who you are, and he is missing out by not having you in his life."

"Thanks." Cam reached for her hand and squeezed gently.

"I've always got your back, baby." She grinned.

Chapter Twenty-One

As Cam finished her drink in the bar, waiting for Michelle to finish her facial and hot stone massage, her mother called and informed her she was ready to be collected.

It was exciting for Cam. Finally having her mother's support and love without restriction was something she had given up dreaming about. Her father was such a stubborn man, and in many ways, she was a lot like him, she knew that. But unlike him, she was able to open her mind to the possibility of being wrong or forgiving, both of which her father had no clue how to do.

As always, when Michelle entered the bar, it took Cam's breath away. Just for a second, she wondered who was lucky enough to take her home, and then it would hit her that it wasn't a dream; Michelle was real and all hers. She noted that several heads turned. Three men seated at the bar had all spotted her wife and were openly ogling her as she made her way past them and over to Cam. Michelle didn't pay them any attention; she only had eyes for Cam.

"All done?" Cam asked, smiling at her. She downed the last of her drink and then stood to kiss her cheek. Making eye contact with the first guy, she winked at him as his eyes rose up from Michelle's arse and met Cam's stare.

"For now," Michelle countered, "but I have a feeling I might need further 'massaging' later." She let herself be guided by Cam's hand resting playfully just above her butt.

Cam leant into her and whispered, "I see. I'll see what I can do about that." She watched as Michelle's eyes darkened with desire. "Mum called, she is ready when we are." She slipped her hand down and across Michelle's ass to take her hand, knowing full well she was staking her claim loud and clear to these guys with ideas in their heads about her wife.

"I still can't believe she is going to come back with us to the States," Michelle continued, unaware of Cam's not-so-subtle point scoring.

"I know, I am still in shock that she has left my father." As Michelle stopped walking and turned to face her, Cam took the opportunity to place a chaste kiss against the corner of her mouth, the men at the bar completely forgotten about. "Are you sure you can cope with my mother visiting?"

Michelle laughed loudly. "Baby, if you can cope with me, I can cope with your mother."

~Yes~

She found a parking spot just along the road from her parents' house and pulled in. As she looked ahead, she groaned and let her head fall back against the headrest.

"What?" Michelle asked looking around. Outside, further along the street, she could see a man, a tall man throwing his arms around and clearly speaking loudly to someone she couldn't quite see yet.

"This will be fun." Cam's sarcastic tone alerted Michelle. "My father is here, and by the look of him he hasn't changed." Sitting there, she took in the scene and cringed. Her father was clearly giving one of his ever-so-boring sermons and letting the entire street know their business.

Her mother, on the other hand, had changed out of her clothes from yesterday and was now sitting on a suitcase in front of the house, surrounded by several other cases and bags. "What is the plan then?" Michelle asked, readying herself for action.

"Well, you can stay here for starters," Cam replied, her eyes still on the scene further down the road.

"Why?" Michelle questioned, a little annoyance causing her voice to deepen a little more than usual. She twisted in her seat to glare at Cam.

Cam felt the stare and turned to face her. She couldn't help the smirk as she noticed the petulant pout on her wife's face. "Because A., I don't want you to have to deal with him, and B., I need you to load the car as quickly as possible as I bring the bags over."

"Okay, as long as I am being of use. I'm not some weak girl in high heels that isn't capable of dealing with an idiot," Michelle retorted with a raise of her eyebrow.

"Well that's good, cos I never married that woman you just described." She leant across and kissed her. "Right, let's get this over with and get out of here. Oh, and by the way, I like the heels."

They both climbed out of the car. Cam crossed the street to her mother, while Michelle opened the trunk, or boot as they called it here in the UK, and readied herself for a quick getaway.

"Mother, are you ready?" Cam asked, completely ignoring her father's presence. Pippa Thomas stood and pulled her suitcase behind her.

On seeing her, Ron Thomas looked flabbergasted. "Oh, I might have known you'd be the instigator in all this." He threw his arms in the air and sneered at her as she grabbed two bags and crossed back to the car. Leaving them with Michelle to pack, she crossed back to get the next.

"You think you can waltz back in here and she can just drop everything to go with you to La La Land?" he continued. Cam grabbed a suitcase and another bag before again crossing the street to deposit both items with Michelle.

"Ron, will you pipe down. It's not her fault!" Pippa shouted at him. "And the entire street doesn't need to hear you."

"Oi, I'm talking to you," he continued, shouting louder, ignoring his wife's protests. This time Cam stopped and glared at him.

"Oh, I am sorry, it has been so long since you did, I assumed you must be talking to someone else," she said smartly, then carried on with collecting two more suitcases.

"Always with the smart mouth. Don't think just cos you've got money now that you can speak to me like that, I am your father."

She stopped at that, turned in the middle of the road, and walked back to him. He stood his ground. "You lost the right to that title a long time ago, long before I had any money. Don't you dare try to blame this on me, you..." she said, pointing a finger in his chest. "*You* are the only one to blame here, you and your stubborn, holier-than-thou, archaic ideals of what everyone else's life should be like. You've been so busy interfering in everyone else's lives that you failed to notice your own one falling apart. You failed as a father and now you've failed as a husband. You lost me and now you're losing mum and you've only yourself to blame. Even Caroline stays away." She glared at him. "You will be one lonely, miserable old man, and you deserve it," she spat, grabbing the cases and stomping across the road as she took them to Michelle.

Michelle opened the door for Pippa to climb into the car and then she waited. Cam stared at her father and shook her head, and then she turned and slid into the driver's seat. Michelle followed suit and they drove away.

Chapter Twenty-Two

Caroline's flat was nice – if you liked half empty and barely lived in, which apparently was how Caroline kept it. Her mother's things were mainly piled up along the thin hallway waiting to be collected and taken to the airport. From Cam's point of view, the place was pokey. Barely room to swing a cat, but then she guessed it was all that Caroline needed. Her work kept her travelling or abroad for long periods, so she probably only spent a few weeks of the year here anyway.

They had enjoyed a pleasant dinner around a tiny table that folded up. A bottle of Chardonnay stood on the table besides two glasses and a cup of tea. The air was thick with unspoken tension. Just saying "I am sorry" was never going to be enough, and it was evident to all parties.

Pippa looked as though she wanted to say something but was holding back. It hadn't been missed by Michelle. "I'm just going to take these plates and start the clean-up," Michelle said, assuming the responsibility of getting things started. Cam smiled up at her as she passed and let her fingers stroke slowly across her wife's shoulders.

"You don't have to do that, Michelle," Pippa tried to argue, a mixed expression of gratefulness and anxiety spreading across her face, but the actress took no notice. Lifting the pile of empty plates and cutlery she replied gently, "It's fine. You two need to talk." Cam stood and collected the drinks, taking them over to the small couch where she flopped down. Her mother took a moment, gathering her own thoughts before she got up, pushing the chair in and moving to sit beside Cam.

She sat side by side with her mother in silence for a while, easing their way into the inevitable. Only the sounds of Michelle running taps, splashing dishes, and the distant hum of traffic passing by on the busy central London street interrupted the silence. But eventually Pippa braved it.

"I am sorry I wasn't here for you when you needed me." Her gaze fell upon Cam and she waited until her daughter turned to look at her before she continued. When she had Cam's attention she said, "I have no excuse good enough for not doing something more. I failed you and I..."

"Mum, it's..."

Pippa Thomas shook her head and raised a hand, placing it gently on her daughter's arm. "No, Camryn, no...it isn't okay." The tears that had threatened before now ran freely. "I did what I always do...I buried my head in the sand and hoped for the best."

"I'm not gonna lie Mum, it hurt. It was all over the news."

"I know, but I don't keep up to date with current affairs. I didn't even know that you were dating anyone, let alone a movie star." She leant in to whisper, "She is lovely, by the way." Cam smiled at her and nodded her agreement.

"I didn't know Michelle had called Caroline...to be honest, it didn't even occur to me to ask if anyone had called my family. But I thought about it these past few days, and how would you have contacted me? I had new numbers and a new address."

"I know, but I'm sorry Camryn. I am so very sorry." They both stared at the wall. a large painting hung there and Cam studied it, gathering her thoughts as her mum continued to talk. "I didn't know how to...I didn't know how to bridge that gap that had grown between us."

"I should have had your number in my phone. I took it out in a moment of petulance I guess," Cam admitted with a thin-lipped smile of regret. Silence sat between them again. There was lost time for both of them that couldn't be gotten back.

The burning question on Pippa's mind though finally found its way to the fore. "Why did she do it?"

Cam shrugged. "Because she's nuts is what I'm going with...we thought it was Michelle that someone was obsessed with. Obviously, we didn't know at the time it was her that was stalking 'Chelle, but in reality, she was just trying to scare her off so that she could sweep in and have me all to herself again." Cam shuddered at the very thought of it

"I never did like her," Pippa stated disdainfully.

"You didn't like her because she was my girlfriend..."

"Not true, your father has that issue...it's never been one for me. I just wanted a happy family, and you never looked happy..."

"How could I? You both disapproved of everything I did." Her voice was raised now. Holding all of this in for so many years, she hadn't realised just how much it had bothered her. "I was never good enough, and being gay was like the cherry on the cake for Dad. I need to know you accept me, Mum. I need to know my wife is never gonna feel awkward or like she doesn't belong, because I will make a choice if I am forced to, and it will always be her."

Pippa took a deep breath and exhaled before she spoke again. She understood her daughter's animosity. Even if the explanation wasn't good enough, she would try. "Do you remember Auntie Celia? You were quite young when she last visited, and she died not long after, so probably not." Cam shook her head. She knew of Auntie Celia, Caroline had talked about her and obviously she had seen family photographs and knew who she was, but she didn't remember her.

Michelle had been listening from the kitchen; these places were so small, it was impossible not to. She heard Cam's warning and slipped into the room feeling loved and prepared to act as referee if needed. Perching down on the arm of the sofa, she placed her own arm around Cam's shoulders and pressed a kiss to Cam's cheek as she too listened to Pippa's story.

"She was your dad's sister, his only sister, and they were very close. When she died, it almost killed your Dad. He struggled to get over it, but he had you and Caroline at home, and so, he threw himself into being the best dad he could be...you remember how close you both were when you were little?"

Camryn nodded; her dad was her hero. They did everything together, and that was why it had been so hard when he shut himself off from her.

"Celia killed herself," Pippa said quietly, her eyes firmly fixed on Camryn.

"God, I didn't know that." Cam shifted in her seat and found Michelle's hand to hold.

Pippa smiled a sad smile. "No, it wasn't talked about. It was easier to tell people that she had had a short illness."

"Why?" Cam asked. She took a sip of her drink and let the heat of the alcohol warm her throat.

"Because the family didn't want to talk about it."

"No, I mean why did she kill herself?" She reached for the bottle of chardonnay and topped up her own glass before offering the same to her mother and then Michelle. Her wife shook her head. She wanted a clear head to hear this story.

"Thank you, yes." Pippa held her glass out and watched as the liquid filled the glass halfway. "When your dad and Celia were younger, he found out something about her that was a secret. Something that nobody else would accept if they knew, but he did...without question, because he loved her...and it didn't matter to him who she loved." She waited for Camryn to catch on.

"Celia was gay?" Cam frowned at this new information. How did that make any sense? Her dad was okay with his sister being gay, but not his daughter?

Pippa nodded and smiled sadly. "Yes, she was a lesbian, but things were different back then." She added quickly, "She couldn't be open about it like you can. Your dad used to try and cover for her as much as he could, but eventually, like most secrets, somebody finds out...Celia couldn't live with the shame and she...one beautiful summer's night she took a handful of pills and drank a bottle of vodka, then she climbed into the bath and when she fell unconscious, she slipped under the water and drowned."

"How awful," Michelle said, sliding down into Cam's lap.

"She left a note...her final words to the world, to your dad, were that she wished above all else that she had been born 'normal,' and that the world was a hateful place for people like her." Pippa sipped her wine and contemplated how to go on. "He isn't a bad man, your father. He just lost his way...when you came out it terrified him that you would end up the same way Celia did. He didn't want his baby girl to have to live in a hateful world where people could hurt you."

"So, he hurt me instead?" she huffed. It wasn't fair, none of it.

"I'm not saying the way he behaved was acceptable or that it really makes any sense. I just want you to have some kind of understanding of why he acted that way." She reached out and took Cam's hand. "He loves you, don't ever think otherwise, he just couldn't handle losing you like he did Celia."

"I get that, maybe...ya know when I was 18, but I'm 35 now. He has had long enough to realise that I'm not Celia. I'm still here...I'm happy."

"And he is stubborn and cantankerous. He doesn't know that he has a route back and so he just cuts himself off. Maybe if you reached out..."

"No." Cam shook her head. "I'm not ready to do that. I've got too much going on right now...things with Michelle are great and we have plans, so many plans that I won't put on hold for him. I've got Kate back and we need to spend some time building our relationship and..."

"And then there is me." Pippa smiled. It was the first time in such a long time that they had actually talked, really talked. With Cam and her father at loggerheads for the entirety of her daughter's twenties, they hadn't had much time together, and she regretted that. "Stuck in the middle. I knew you needed to go and find your own way in life, but I couldn't just leave him." She smiled and nodded to Michelle. "Just like you would choose Michelle now…I stuck by him, hoping he would see his faults and reach out. But the more I tried to push him, the more stubborn about it he became until it got to the point where my choice changed." She reached for Cam's hand. "I missed my daughter."

"We will get there, Mum."

Chapter Twenty-Three

The last day of their trip arrived, and everything was finalised for the return journey. The original plan to just fly back into LAX from Heathrow went out of the window when Pippa agreed to come with them. Now, they had more luggage than Cam would have thought possible, so a private jet was now being readied instead. Not that Cam was complaining about that part. Comfort on a flight that long was essential in her mind. It was the last-minute packing of her own clothes that was the burden. Her mother had offered to help, but Michelle was having none of it, having asked Cam to start doing it two days before.

"If she had put the dirty clothes into a laundry bag at least, then I would have finished it for her, but no...instead she was playing around, so..." Michelle turned from Pippa's amused face towards Camryn's pouting one. "You can finish packing and then we-"

The sound of Cam's phone ringing loudly from her pocket caused a smug grin to spread itself across Cam's face as she recognised the new ringtone she had set for Kate. "Saved by the bell!" she hollered as she swiped across the screen to answer. "Yep," she said cheerfully into the handset, tucking it into the crook of her neck as she tossed the jumper she was halfway through folding into the case. Michelle groaned and fell backwards onto the bed in frustration.

"Please, Michelle, let me do it," Pippa said, smiling when Michelle nodded in acquiescence. "You can make her suffer tomorrow," she laughed wickedly, and Michelle understood where Cam's sense of humour came from.

"Hi Cam, it's me," a rather subdued Kate said on her end of the phone.

"Hey, what's up?" She put the jumper down and straightened up, taking the phone in her hand to listen properly.

"I was wondering if I could come over. Catch up with you before you go?"

Cam checked her watch. They still had several hours before their car was picking them up. It would be nice to say a proper goodbye before they left.

"Yeah sure, I'll order some lunch in."

"Sounds great, see you in an hour then."

~Yes~

With bags and cases finally piled up by the door ready to go, the flat felt somewhat empty. It had never bothered Cam before; the place had just been somewhere to sleep on the few occasions that she was in town, nothing more than a hotel room, but now – now it felt like a home, and she would miss it a little.

She was dragged from her thoughts when the bell rang announcing Kate's arrival. Jumping up, she dashed down the hall and hit the entry button on the gates so that Kate could drive in and park.

It didn't take long for Kate to ride up the lift and knock gently on the door. Cam swung it open with a big grin and was halted dead in her tracks, instantly aware of Kate's red-rimmed eyes and tearstained cheeks.

"Hey, what's wrong?" Her voice automatically softened to her friend's distress.

"Oh nothing, I..." She paused to think. "Michael and I have split up," she confessed. "And you're leaving, and I just..." She sobbed. "...needed to see you before you left me too."

"Come on, get in here," Cam said, opening the door fully and tugging her inside. "Why have you and Michael split?"

"We agreed that it just wasn't heading where either of us wanted and so, he said it was probably best to just end it now. And he is right, but I...oh I don't know, I just wasn't expecting it right now I guess."

"I am sorry, it sucks I know, but at least you're now free to pursue the right person." They both sat together on the sofa.

"Yeah, I guess so, maybe it is time to make a lot of changes in my life," Kate considered. She gazed out of the window and watched a pigeon float by, its wings spread wide as it glided with ease over the city below.

Pippa popped her head around the door, smiling at Kate. "Cup of tea?"

"Yes, please Ma. You know the answer is always yes to that one." Cam smiled sadly and tilted her head towards her friend. "I think Kate needs one."

She sat quietly for a moment, contemplating her friend. She looked pensive as she continued to stare out of the window. Cam considered her for a moment longer, how easily they had just fallen back into their friendship. Yeah, it needed work still, but on the whole, it was simple with Kate.

"Okay, I have an idea," Cam said, finally coming up with a solution, "and you can say no of course, but...come with us to LA."

"I guess I could do with a holiday," Kate considered as she turned to smile sadly at Pippa. The older woman carrying two mugs of freshly brewed tea for them. She set it down on the table in front of them and smiled back. "Sounds like a lovely idea, I could do with the company."

"Well yeah, you could do that or..." Cam grinned as she sat forward, lifting the cup. She took a sip of her tea and winced at how hot it still was. "Look, I just bought a gym, I need someone to help run it."

Kate stared at her. "You're offering me a job?"

"Yeah, I am, if you want it? You're more qualified than I am!" She continued to grin, her mother following; it was infectious.

Kate was astounded. Just a few days ago they weren't even on speaking terms with each other, and now Cam was inviting her to work for her, move abroad with her and her family. It was surreal.

Decision-making wasn't Kate's forte. She liked to think things through; change didn't sit too well with her. "Can I think about it?"

"Yes, of course," Cam said realising it *was* a big deal. A huge deal actually. Having money makes a lot of difference in the confidence to make decisions. Back when she was just like Kate, the idea of just packing up her life and moving would have terrified her into staying put. Now though, with her bank account behind her, it was a whole lot easier to just do something. If it went wrong, she could afford to fix it.

"When would you need to know by?"

Cam checked her watch again. "About 3 hours?" she laughed. "I have a jet arranged for this evening, so if you say yes then you can jump on board with us, or of course fly out at a later date."

Kate couldn't help but laugh. "Jesus Cam, 3 hours?" She felt her heart race at the implication.

"Well, it will be less now you've wasted 3 minutes." She chuckled.

Kate reached into her pocket and pulled out a hairband. Running her fingers through her hair, she quickly pulled it through the band and tied it in place, out of the way. "Hang on. You are really offering me a job in LA?"

"Yes!" Cam nodded. "You'd have complete control of the gym and businesses associated with it, like the café and instructors for classes and stuff.

Kate thought for a moment longer. "Where will I live?"

"You can live at my place," Michelle said, entering the room and overhearing the conversation. She took a seat on the arm of Cam's chair and relaxed back against as she leant in towards Cam. "It's empty at the moment since I moved in with Cam."

Kate looked around the room at three expectant faces peering back at her. All three were wide-eyed and half smiling as they waited. Michelle bit her bottom lip and Cam leant forward, elbows on her knees. Pippa held her mug between both hands, unsure whether to take a sip or not.

"Yes. Okay, I am going to do it," she said quickly, before she changed her own mind. Cam jumped up from her seat so fast that Michelle fell into it and Pippa almost lost her tea. Kate laughed at the sight in front of her as nervous excitement bubbled up inside of her too.

Cam threw her arms around her and hugged her hard. "Go, get packing." She laughed, pushing her out of the door. "Just meet us at the airfield by seven. I'll text you the details."

Chapter Twenty-Four

For Pippa Thomas and Kate Morris, it was a day of firsts for both of them. Traveling on a private jet was surreal, and the entire journey was a serious of gasps and wows. Cam had smiled from her seat next to Michelle, remembering the first time she had done this. One of the women she had dated, Amanda, had put her in touch with Tom. He was her travel guru and could organise flights and accommodation like a magician.

She was still a little unsure of herself and her newfound riches, but she needed to get to Greece quickly. She was negotiating for the villa she wanted to buy and knew that a personal appearance was more likely to swing it with the traditional Greek owner than a series of emails and phone calls. "Tom, it's Cam Thomas," she said into the handset. "Hey there, what can I do for you today?" he answered, his voice full of confidence and bravado.

"So, I need to get to Greece." Before she finished speaking she could hear him tapping away on a keyboard.

"When by?"

She winced a little; it was really short notice. "Uh, tomorrow?"

Unfazed by the request, he said, "Okay, lemme see what we can do." Another series of taps on the keyboard and he blew out a breath that culminated in a short whistle. "Alright, well the bad news is, I can get you on a flight, but it doesn't leave till tomorrow afternoon, which would mean arriving late in Greece."

"And the good news?" She really hoped she could head to the airport tonight and be there tomorrow afternoon, local time.

"If money is no object, then I can rent you a private jet?"

She glanced over at her wife as she continued to sleep, oblivious to the plane landing and now taxiing along the runway. She gently shook her awake, smiling at the look of confusion on her sleepy face. "We're here," she whispered as Michelle rubbed her eyes and stretched. Cam removed her seatbelt and stood up. Her mother and Kate were both in the process of organising their things for when the steward would signal that the door was ready to open. "Okay, shall we get going?"

"Seriously, this is how you roll now?" Kate laughed as they descended the steps down from the jet. The heat of the night air was a welcome hello to the returning couple. Leaving a cold and damp London afternoon behind, it was strange to now be walking out onto tarmac with a warm breeze wrapping around them. A stretch limo waited in the darkness for them, lights dimmed. A driver stood in full uniform and as they neared the vehicle, she opened the door and held it for them. Every one of them thanked her as they climbed in and took a comfortable seat.

"'Fraid so. Better get used to it if ya gonna be hanging out with me." Cam smiled. Michelle noted that her accent was much more pronounced since her visit home to London. She had always found the way Cam spoke arousing, but now there was just a touch more to it. Maybe she would have Cam read to her later, something sensual and erotic, or maybe just a newspaper. She had a feeling that it wouldn't matter what Cam said, as long as she was speaking.

They sped through the streets of LA out towards the coast with the window open, all of them lost somewhere in their own thoughts. Kate and Pippa were on a new adventure, and it included Camryn. They all had the opportunity to build bridges and create better relationships than the ones they had had. Michelle was enjoying having these new people in her life too, people who helped to join the dots of who Camryn was. She had never doubted Cam's honesty or sincerity, but she knew there was so much more to this woman that she still had to learn, and she liked that idea. She hoped there would always be more to find out about Cam, and that Cam would always be finding new things that she loved about her. For Cam, it was all so surreal, one of those pinch yourself moments that she had now and then whenever she considered how different her life was now.

~Yes~.

Arriving at the house, Cam opened the door and led them inside. "Tea?" Cam asked, dumping her bag at the bottom of the stairs as everyone piled in behind her. Their luggage would be delivered in the morning; for now all any of them had was a small bag with essentials. Cam's mother insisted on a change of clothes at the very least. Kate had firmly agreed. They both filed past their hosts and headed towards the door in front of them that led to the kitchen.

"Did you let Maria know we have guests?" Michelle asked Cam when they were alone. She had completely forgotten until just now that the housekeeper would want to know in advance of impending guests.

"Yep, all sorted," Cam said, reaching for her. She could hear her mother babbling on to Kate about the size of the kitchen and the gadgets. "Did I tell you today just how much I love you?"

Michelle smiled and leaned forward to kiss her. "No," she whispered against her lips, ghosting over them with her own as she waited for Cam's usual reply.

"Oh, how remiss of me." She caught Michelle's bottom lip between her own and held it there just a moment before continuing. "I love you more today than I ever did yesterday." Michelle deepened the kiss without prompting.

"God, I love you so much," she gasped as they separated.

"Great, maybe later you can show me." Cam winked.

"Uh huh, I guess that can be arranged." She was taller than Cam today, wearing her 4-inch heels, with Cam was in flats as usual. She dipped her head and brought their lips together again.

~Yes~

They found Kate in the kitchen with Cam's mother, sitting at the breakfast bar drinking tea. They both wore a similar look on their faces: apprehension and excitement all rolled into one strange look that made them both appear dazed.

"So, how we all doing?" Cam asked brightly, a little too brightly for this time of night, but she was happy.

"Well, I have to say, Camryn, that I am a little overwhelmed," her mother replied first, along with a nod of agreement from Kate.

"Okay."

"Just how rich are you?" she asked, completely seriously. "Private jets and limousines? And this house? I can hear the sea, Camryn." She paused. "It's all just so..." She paused again to think of the word she needed, but Kate answered for her.

"Flabbergasting."

Cam had to giggle. This was Cam's life now and on the whole, she was used to it, but those pinch yourself moments always left her feeling overwhelmed, so she got where they were coming from. There had been no headline when she had won her money. She chose anonymity and only her financial advisor and the bank actually knew the real figure of her worth at any one time. Michelle and her folks had a rough idea, but even Cam didn't know the exact figure as it fluctuated with markets and financial goings on in the world.

"When I last looked, my bank account said-"

"Oh Camryn, I don't really want to know. I am just, well it's flabbergasting, like Kate said." She laughed a little. "It will just take a while to get used to the idea that my child can buy anything she wants. And it's a little daunting that I am destitute and need to rely on you financially," she then added. "It isn't something I ever envisaged happening."

Cam hadn't realised how much of a big deal that might be to her mother. As far as she was concerned, it was just money. She had money and her mother didn't, she hadn't considered pride. If roles were reversed, then she already knew that she too would hate any form of charity.

She was going to need a solution, but for now it was late, and they had just flown half way across the world, and she was tired. She wanted to sleep in her own bed and snuggle against her wife as she fell asleep wrapped up with her.

"Mum, I know it's weird, but we will work it out, alright? And the same for you, Kate. I know it's all a lot of change and we need to work on the finer details, but for now, please just accept my ability to afford whatever you need." They all nodded in agreement. "Great, I need to go to bed. Come on, I'll show you both to your rooms."

Cam led the way. She noticed that her own bag had gone from the foot of the stairs. Michelle must have taken it up. Just the thought of Michelle waiting upstairs for her made her feel lighter as she climbed the steps.

"Okay, Kate, you're in here." She opened the door to a perfectly lovely guest room. There was a queen-sized bed and bespoke, matching bedroom furniture. It was a simple room, if you were used to living in a 5-star hotel. "The bathroom is just through there." She pointed to another door a few feet away. "Just be aware that its shared between you and the room that Mum will be in."

"I am sure we will cope." Kate grinned.

When Cam opened the door to Pippa's room, she walked in and dropped her mum's bag to the floor. As Pippa followed in behind, there was an audible gasp.

"Camryn, this room is lovely."

The bed was huge compared to UK standards, and there was a beautiful lace throw on the bed, with 6 plump pillows. The walls were painted in a light pink hue that was accented by deep red curtains. There was a plush deep pile carpet on the floor that was the same red as the drapes. Large pieces of dark antique furniture were placed strategically around the room, but it didn't even begin to fill the space available. She could put the room she had shared with Ron for the last 40 years into this room twice and still had some space to spare.

"If you need anything or want to change anything, just let me or Michelle know." Cam's face beamed in happiness. "Or Maria, you'll love Maria." The smile faltered a little as she thought of the diminutive Mexican woman that had replaced this one standing in front of her for the past few years. Just briefly she was reminded of the sadness that she had held within her.

Her thoughts were interrupted, however, when her mother began to speak. "I don't think it needs anything. I am going to go to bed and in the morning, I'll unpack," she said, kissing her daughter's cheek. "Thank you, Cam."

"You're welcome." She turned to leave but was stopped by her mother's hand touching her arm.

"Camryn? Do you think maybe soon we could talk some more, about what Jessica did to you?"

Cam took a step back, away from the question, her eyes plunging to stare at the floor for a moment. She hadn't expected that question at all; they had talked back in London, and Cam had naively thought that maybe her mother was satisfied by that.

"Sure, if you want to," she said, nodding.

"I'd like to yes, I'd like to know more about what happened to you."

"Okay," she said, quietly whispering good night as she left and closed the door behind her. Once outside in the hallway she had to stop and catch her breath. *God, would it never end? Was this what her life would always be about?*

She was quiet as she entered her bedroom, their bedroom, her sanctuary. The one place she knew she would find her anchor, the woman who held her heart with a surety she had never understood before.

Michelle was already in bed, reading a magazine, her hair loose around her face, reading glasses perched on her nose. She was beautiful and calm and everything Cam needed her to be right now. She was wearing a lavender-coloured night dress, something silky and strappy. It left her shoulders bare and dipped low on her chest, revealing a tiny mole. It complemented her skin tone perfectly. As she looked up, she noticed Cam looking at her.

"What's wrong?" she asked, immediately sitting forward and placing her magazine to the side.

Cam closed her eyes and leant back against the door as she closed it. "Mum wants to talk about Jessica again."

"Oh, and you're not feeling too great about that?"

Cam rubbed her face with her hand.

"Come here," Michelle commanded, patting the bed beside her as she pulled back the covers and swung her legs around. Cam did as she was told and crossed the floor, but she didn't sit down. Instead she stood in front of her. Michelle's thighs parted, and Cam took the step forward to where she wanted to be.

"I feel like...it's never ending ya know?" Cam admitted sadly. She felt her shirt rise up a little as warm lips found a place to kiss. "Every time I think I've got my head around it, I realise I haven't.

"I know. Maybe it will always be there, in the background." Michelle was tugging at her belt now, unhooking and pulling it free from the loops that held it in place. "Maybe if you talk about it some more, it will have less of a hold on you," she said as her fingers deftly undid the button and slid the zipper downwards. Michelle gripped the waist of her jeans and tugged them loose and down her thighs. "If you don't want to talk about it, then I can explain anything she wants to know about," she continued as her fingers lifted Cam's shirt up and encouraged her to pull it off. Braless, she stood in just her underwear and felt warm lips press against her abdomen once more. She closed her eyes and tried to lose herself in the sensations.

Skilful fingers hooked her panties and began the process of sliding them down her toned legs. Michelle sat further back on the bed and pulled Cam with her.

"I know that I want to make love to you," Cam said, holding herself up so she could look at her. Michelle reached up and hooked her hair behind her ear.

"You can," she answered earnestly.

"You're tired though," Cam reasoned, trying to control her arousal. Although, if Michelle kept this up, she would easily give in.

Sensing the chance to win this battle, Michelle kissed her quickly. "I slept on the plane." Her voice dropped to that low and sexy husk that Cam liked so much. When she resumed the kiss, she was met by Cam with as much gusto.

As Michelle tried to sit up again to pull her night dress off, Cam stopped her. "Leave it on," she whispered and pushed her back down on the bed, following her as she went. "I like the way you feel under this," she admitted as her hands roamed and smoothed over the material to feel the warmth of her wife's body beneath it. She felt the dip of her hips as her palm travelled the plane of her abdomen, sweeping upwards to smoothly encase the swell of her breast. It all felt so new and exciting to Cam's touch.

As she lowered herself, she kissed the crease of Michelle's neck, working her way up towards her ear and back down again, moving lower. Her hand skimmed the surface of her until her fingers wound into her hair. She felt Michelle arch against her as her mouth moved to suck a firm nipple through the material that concealed it.

Her other hand slid lower and cupped between parted thighs, expensive silk material the only barrier between them. A barrier Cam was enjoying. Gentle panting and soft groans grew steadily in volume and cadence. The silk soaked easily with Michelle's slick arousal as Cam pressed her fingers more firmly against her, stimulating the need that was growing within Michelle, building deep within the pit of her stomach. Cam was hypnotised by the sight and sound of her. She would never grow tired of loving this woman.

Chapter Twenty-Five

When you are a movie star you can afford a certain standard of living. You can afford to live in the best neighbourhoods, in the nicest house, and you can fill it will the stuff that most people only dream about. That was Michelle's house. The place that Kate could only dream about.

So, when you offer that house to a friend of your wife to live in, when she has just split from her boyfriend and moved her life halfway across the world on a whim, well, you have to expect a certain amount of disbelief will be their reaction to seeing it.

So far Kate Morris had failed to speak at all. They had arrived at Michelle's house around 20 minutes ago. Walking Kate around the property had taken around ten of those minutes. A further five were taken up by wandering the garden and outside space.

Three bedrooms all with bathrooms and an open planned living room and kitchen bigger than Kate's flat back in London were already enough to cause the speechless reaction. However, there were bi-folding doors that led to a patio, that then led to the outdoor pool. An outdoor pool! The only time Kate had been in an outdoor pool was when the school had taken them on a trip to the local lido. It wasn't an experience she wanted to remember, as the water was freezing cold and the sky overcast. But here, in all this sunshine, she could swim all the time.

She looked around once more. Everything was all so much bigger than anything she could have dared to dream of while living in in the UK. Cam sat down on the flagstone step and waited her out. Michelle looked amused as she too watched the flustered Englishwoman move around the space.

Several times Kate looked as though she was about to speak, but then didn't, her mind finding something else to question and focus on. Eventually though, she turned to Michelle and then to Cam. "This isn't a joke, is it?" She looked around the room once more. Her long, dark hair, tied up in a ponytail, swished back and forth with the movement.

"Not a joke," Cam said, smiling. "And we're not throwing you out, you can stay with us longer if you want to, but, I mean, it just sits here empty since Michelle moved in with me." It had only been a couple of days, but Cam wanted to get Kate settled as soon as possible. An army of cleaners had been sent in to ready it for Kate's inspection. Cam was excited to show her friend and have her feel at home here in LA.

"And you seriously don't want me to pay any rent for it?" she clarified for the umpteenth time since they had spoken seriously about it.

"Nope, just bills," Cam confirmed. "It's paid for, there is no mortgage."

Kate chewed her lip as she considered the information again. "And you're going to pay me $60,000 dollars to manage your gym?" Cam had gone over the finer points of the contract earlier in the day.

"Sounds about right," Cam agreed. "I'll need to get Jeff on the case to get you a working visa, but he will work it out." Her lawyer was a magician when it came to getting things done.

Kate flopped down next to Cam on the step and nudged her shoulder with her own. "It's going to take a while for me to get my head around this, Cam," she said honestly.

"I know, but once you do...Bobby Pedrosa lives three doors down and opposite." Cam jutted her chin towards the house. "Greta Donaldson lives there when she is in LA."

"Get the hell out."

"Seriously, hobnobbing with the stars now, Kate." Cam laughed at the shocked expression on her friend's face. "Bobby Pedrosa?"

Michelle laughed. "Uh huh, I could introduce you if you like?"

Kate shook her head, laughing, "It's kind of crazy, ya know that right?" Kate said. Her life had literally changed overnight.

Cam burst out laughing. Nodding, she agreed. "Yeah, it kind of is."

~Yes~

It wasn't quite so simple back at the beach house a few days later. Walking through the door, the raised voice instantly alerted them to a problem. Maria was ranting in Spanish. Pots were clanging and banging down on the surfaces before being picked up and banged down somewhere else.

Michelle looked towards Cam for an answer. She shrugged and continued down the hallway towards the noise, leaving Michelle to watch after her. She stood just inside the doorway and observed as her housekeeper got whatever was bothering her out of her system.

She had cupboard doors open and was moving things back and forth, all the while mumbling one minute before she found something else that annoyed her, and she would throw her hands up into the air and shout louder to God to help save her from something Cam couldn't understand but got the impression might be a life sentence for murdering someone.

"Maria? What's up?" The smell in the room was amazing, and Cam could feel her stomach rumble at the idea of eating whatever was cooking in the oven. But before she got anywhere near what was in that pot, she needed to find the cause of this. She had never seen Maria so unhappy and upset.

The Mexican woman gasped and then crossed herself as she realised Cam was there. "Oh, Camryn, you scare me!" She stood up and took a deep breath to calm herself. Cam took the opportunity to move into the room and crossed the space to be nearer to her.

She placed a caring arm around Maria's shoulders and pulled her in for an embrace. "Is something wrong?"

Maria shook her head. "No, I am fine." She pulled a cloth from her waistband and started rubbing at the countertop, cleaning it to within an inch of its life. She was fooling nobody with the charade.

"Well, I don't think you are fine at all," Cam said, taking hold of her shoulders. She turned her so they were face to face again. "I don't like seeing you this upset."

Maria placed the cloth down on the sideboard and looked up at Cam, sighing. "Your mother," was all she said. Cam dropped her arms to her sides and nodded.

"Go on."

"I just...this is my kitchen. I cook, I clean, I put things where I want," she said, her finger pointing at the things she was talking about, including the cause of all the noise: the pots and pans. "She come here and move all my things, cooking, cleaning..." She trailed off, something left unsaid.

"I'm sure she's just trying to help. I'll speak to her about putting things back where she found them." Maria nodded, seemingly satisfied, but Cam wasn't convinced. "Is that all you want to say?"

Maria pursed her lips and considered her next move. She had never shied away from telling Camryn what she thought, but maybe this wasn't her business. "She's your mother, it's not my place."

"Your place? Maria, I wanna know what you think. Your opinion is important to me." Her words were sincere; Maria knew how much Camryn thought of her.

Maria straightened up and held her chin up. "Okay, I don't like it." Seeing the confused look on Cam's face she added, "You nearly die, and where she is? You here all by yourself for all this time, where she is?" Cam could sense the anger. This woman who had, for the most part, played the role of her mother for the last two years had every right to be angry at this turn of events.

"You're right, she wasn't here. You were." She tugged Maria into her arms and hugged her again. "I know that. Don't think just because my mum and I are working on our relationship, that it means I don't need you." Pulling back to look at her, she added, "I love you, Maria, just as if you were my mother, because you've been that person for me."

Maria nodded, seemingly satisfied for now. "Dinner will be ready in thirty minutes."

Chapter Twenty-Six

Filming on *Medical Diaries* restarted, and Michelle returned to the studio again. She had missed it. Her colleagues were like a family now. They'd been on set together now for years, but every hiatus before now had felt like a lifetime until she could return. She would keep herself busy with as many projects as Janice could get her involved with to make the time go faster. Not this time; having Camryn in her life had made the all the difference, and she had enjoyed every minute of not working. Her entire life up till now had been concentrated on her career.

So, as much as she would miss spending all day with Cam, she also couldn't wait to get back into the groove and find out where her character would be heading this season.

It would be like a well-worn and practised routine for the first couple of days. She would be going through scripts and practising lines, getting to know new cast members. It was easy and fun.

With such a big cast and crew on a show like this, the bonus was that she wasn't required every day on set. However, with her recent time away dealing with the fallout from Jessica, she knew her character would now be given a good storyline to make the most of the media interest. She didn't mind; it was all part of the game they played in Hollywood. She had just been grateful for the support from the studio this past year, but she just couldn't get it out of her head that she wanted to have a baby.

Having a child had never been on her radar before. She had barely thought about it because she had always been so wrapped up in her career. When Robbie and Jen had had Zac, there had been a brief moment of being a little broody, but it had passed the minute Janice had called with a prospective part in a major blockbuster.

She hadn't gotten the part, but she hadn't thought about having kids again either. Even when Dylan came along, she didn't feel that same broodiness that she had before. Now though, it was all she could think about. She wanted a child, with Cam.

~Yes~

"Cam?" Erin said as her boss strolled through the doors to OUT. She wasn't alone either. "I wasn't expecting you in today."

"Hey Erin. This is my mum and my friend, Kate," she said, pointing to each woman in turn. "I'm just showing them around." She then turned to Pippa and Kate. "This is Erin, she is the manager here at OUT, and she's a good friend too, so you'll probably see her often."

"Lovely to meet you both, how are you enjoying your visit so far?" Erin asked, reaching forward to shake hands with each of them. She raised an eyebrow at Cam, surprised. Was this *the* Kate? Cam smirked and nodded slowly.

"They're not just visiting...well, I hope they're not." Cam smiled. "They're staying for now. Kate is going to run the gym for me."

If Erin was shocked at the news, she managed to hide it well. "Wow, well that's just great."

"Yeah, it was an offer I couldn't really turn down." Kate grinned, enjoying the tour Cam had given them so far. She hadn't expected to love LA this much already, but Cam had been taking them around town and introducing them to people and showing them places off the beaten track.

Cam led them further into the bar and found Angie waiting for Fran. She ordered drinks for them all and led them towards a booth.

"This is lovely, Camryn," Pippa said, taking a seat and shuffling along so that Kate could slide in beside her. "You must be really proud of yourself."

Cam blushed. "Yeah, well it has been my passion these last couple of years and with Erin managing, it's going from strength to strength. I am happy with it."

"And how did you meet?" Pippa asked, turning to Angie.

"Uh, oh, uh," she stammered, unsure what to say. 'Your daughter and I had a night of unadulterated sex and we've been friends ever since' didn't seem like the right response.

Cam chuckled and jumped in to spare her friends blushes. "We met when I first arrived in LA. Angie and I went out on a date and we've been friends ever since." Cam winked across the table at her pal. Her mother wouldn't ask for any further details.

"I see, well that's nice." Pippa smiled at her and then took a sip of her drink.

"So, I was thinking once we've finished our drink here that we could go and get some lunch in this really great Mediterranean restaurant I found recently," Cam said to Angie. "You and Fran wanna join us?"

"Sure, why not?"

While they were talking and catching up, Cam's phone rang. Her face lit up as she saw the image of Michelle beaming out at her from the screen. "Hello," she said, "You okay?"

"Can we have a baby now?" Michelle blurted out in reply before laughing at herself. "I'm sorry, let me start again. Hello."

"Uh, hi." She shifted Angie from her seat so that she could slide out and move somewhere a little more private. "I'll be right back," she told the group. "So, what? You want to have a baby, right now?" Flustered would be an appropriate word for how Cam felt right now. This was not the direction she expected a conversation with Michelle to go today.

"Yes. I know we said that we would enjoy life a little first, but Cam...I just can't stop thinking about it."

Cam brushed her fingers through her hair as she paced the empty dance floor. It wasn't a bad idea or something she was completely against, but she had had plans for them. Taking some more trips together and partying, lots of partying. A baby now would change all of that. "Alright, look we can't have this conversation on the phone. Let's talk tonight, what time will you be home?"

"Really, you're not against the idea then?" Michelle breathed a sigh of relief.

"No, I'm not against the idea, it's just...Let's talk later, okay?"

"Yes!" She sounded excited, and Cam smiled. "Eight, I'll be home around eight."

Chapter Twenty-Seven

The bedroom was still warm from the heat of the day. There was music drifting lazily across the room from Michelle's docking centre on the dresser. Next to it sat a large gilded frame with a photograph of them taken by a paparazzi photographer. Cam had bought the image and had it printed. Sitting cross-legged in the centre of the bed waiting for Michelle, Cam let her mind wander. She had spent the last half an hour up here by herself, just thinking.

Kate had invited Pippa around for dinner after Cam had hinted at needing some time to speak with Michelle about something important. She hadn't questioned it, and Cam was grateful for that. Her mind had been elsewhere all afternoon since speaking with her wife. When her mother had broached the subject, she had laughed it off, but it had lain heavy with her these past few hours.

She heard the sweep of the door open against the carpet and Michelle almost glided in, a vision of beauty that made Cam's heart beat faster every time she saw her. She looked tired, but she was smiling at Cam, their eyes plunging into one another. She looked casual in her sweatpants and jumper, though Cam knew the outfit had cost a small fortune. It didn't matter, Cam was enthralled with her.

"Hey." Michelle offered a small smile of apology. "I...I'm sorry about earlier, that was unfair of me to..."

"Yes."

"I know, and I'll make it up to you," she continued as she kicked off her sneakers and moved up to the edge of the bed. "I just got so..."

"Yes," Cam repeated, her eyes never leaving the face that neared, readying herself for the ultimate kiss.

"We have lots of time to just..." The brunette climbed onto the bed on her knees in front of Cam.

"Yes, I said, yes, Michelle."

Michelle stopped moving and stared at her wife. "Yes? You mean..."

"Yes! I dunno how many more ways I can say yes, but yes." She nodded. "If you're really sure that this is what you want, then yes. Let's have a baby."

"Oh my God," Michelle squealed and threw her arms around Cam's neck, forcing her backwards. "Thank you." She peppered Cam's face with kisses before finding her mouth and expressing her thanks much more passionately.

"But..." Cam said, stopping Michelle in an instant from unbuttoning her shirt. She leaned up to look at her. "First things first."

"Okay, what's that?"

"We have been married for a month now, well, five weeks."

"Yes." Michelle grinned, remembering the day she became Mrs Thomas.

"Right, well you need to remember that, and there are the practicalities of it all too, it's not as simple for us." Michelle sat up, allowing Cam to do the same. "You'll have to speak with Janice. What will happen with your job? Have you thought about that? They've already given you so much time off when I was injured."

"I know they did and the answer is, I don't know. I'll speak with Janice and Doug. I'll sound them out and see what we can do...but Cam, if it means I stop working for a while, then I am ready for that. I want a baby, I want our baby." She fixed her eyes with those of her wife and waited.

"Even if it means losing this job?"

Michelle nodded, barely containing her excitement. She bit her bottom lip.

"Even if it means you never get another acting job?"

There was a small hesitation, but then she nodded again.

"I just want you to be sure. Nothing changes for me. I can agree to this and it makes no real difference to my life. A few plans go out the window, but nothing really changes. I'll get up, I'll work around the baby and you. But for you, you could be giving up everything you've worked for."

"You don't want to do this, do you?" Michelle frowned, her eyes misting over. Cam patted the space between her legs and Michelle flopped into it, pressing herself against Cam's torso.

"I do, I want it." She kissed the side of her head. "I just, I don't think we should rush into it. It's a huge decision."

Michelle thought for a moment. "What if we agree to work everything out and put everything in place so that *if* we still feel the same way in say, six months, then we go for it?"

Cam kissed her again. "I think that sounds like a plan I can get on board with." Michelle turned in her arms. "In the meantime, I was thinking of taking a trip at the weekend. You still have Monday and Tuesday off?"

"I do, where are we going to go?"

"I found something online that I wanna take a look at."

"Camryn, stop teasing...what did you find?"

"A holiday home by the lake, Lake Tahoe?"

Chapter Twenty-Eight

Michelle hadn't been to Janice Rashbrook's office since her meltdown over Camryn. She had been sitting in this very same chair when she had finally admitted that she was in love. She glanced around the room. There wasn't much different from then. A couple of new photographs of Janice's latest clients adorned the walls, and she was pretty sure that it was a new rug on the floor over by the couch.

"So, this is a surprise," Janice said, sitting back in her chair like a woman that owned the world. "What are you after?"

"I'm not after anything. I thought I'd just come down here and have a chat, catch up." She used her most dazzling smile, the one that usually worked on anyone she gave it to. But not Janice.

"Uh huh, a catch-up. Right, well, as a matter of fact, it's good timing. I have a job offer for you, some new advertising thing for some such." She was pulling and pushing paper around on her desk. "It's here somewhere."

"Okay, look, Janice...I do have something..."

"Ah-ha, here it is. It's super cool and exactly what you were asking about doing more of...they wanna use that TV show, *Survivor*? That's the premise of the ad, so you'll be..."

"Flinging myself off stuff, driving fast cars, and being thrown around a lot?"

"Yes! Exactly that, fun huh?"

"No."

"No? what do you mean, no? This is what you were asking for!" Janice sat forward in her chair and glared across the desk.

"I know, it's what I wanted last year, and I am happy to look at it if it's going to be done now. But..." She paused to take a breath for a little bit of dramatic effect. "I...Cam and I, we've talked and I, well...the thing is that I...want to have a baby."

"A baby?" Janice exclaimed.

Michelle nodded. "And Cam has agreed..."

"Are you out of your mind?" Janice stood and walked around the desk. "Did you get a bang on the head?! Right now, you are one of the most talked about actors in Hollywood. Rightly or wrongly, falling in love with a woman and then with what happened to Cam...you'd be a fool to get pregnant now."

"I don't..."

"I have offers coming out of my ears for you right now. Most of them I turn down because I know you won't leave Cam to go and film, but..."

"Jan, can I actually get a word in?"

She held her hands up. "Sure."

"So, we want to have a child, that much we agree on. However, we also agreed that we would wait six months before we tried."

Janice ran a hand through her short hair and rubbed her face. "Michelle, do you understand what you're doing?"

"Yes." She smiled. "I do...me and Cam, we want this. I want you to sound everyone out. Find out where I will stand if and when I get pregnant."

Her agent sighed, walked back behind her desk, and sat down again. She leant her elbows on the desk and clasped her hands in front of her face, like a woman in prayer. Finally, she nodded. "Okay, if that's what you want then...I'll be ready to deal with the studio. In the meantime, I have some interviews lined up."

"Thank you." She stood up to leave. Her work here was done.

"Michelle," Janice called out, sitting back in her chair once more. "I hope it all works out. You'll make a great mom."

~Yes~

Loud rock music blasted out of the speaker system. Cam recognised the song, an old one from the 90s, but she couldn't put a name to the band. The bar would be closed for another three hours, and she was hoping to get some paperwork done before heading out to dinner with Michelle. Nearing the bar, she could see Erin on the dance floor letting loose and singing. Singing really well.

She pulled up a bar stool and sat down quietly to watch the impromptu show. It took a full two minutes before Erin finally noticed she had an audience.

Clapping, Cam jumped down. "Wow, where have you been hiding that?"

Erin was blushing, but she grinned wildly underneath the purple hair that didn't seem to have any style but was perfectly suited to her. "Well, not so much hiding. I just...anyway, why are you here? I thought I had the place to myself for an hour."

"So I see," Cam chuckled. "Is this a regular performance?"

"About three times a week." She giggled.

"You need a band," Cam said in all seriousness.

"Oh, I had one of those a long time ago." She smiled ruefully as they climbed the stairs to the office. "We never made it."

"I think you should get another one, come on, it would be great!" Cam argued. "And you could have Sunday nights."

Erin stopped on the top step. "What?"

"Get a band together and I'll give you Sunday nights..."

"You're actually serious, aren't you?" she said, following Cam into the office.

"I am, you're really good. Come on, it will be fun. I can be founding member of your fan club!"

Chapter Twenty-Nine

Getting home earlier than expected, Cam took a quick run in the evening sun along the shore. Carrie followed behind. It wasn't often now that she took one of her security team with her, but when she ventured off on her own then one of them would tag along regardless. Sometimes she would go out just to make them follow her, turning it into a game rather than get annoyed with it, but it was becoming more and more unnecessary.

A 5k round trip had her home back in view within 45 minutes. Sweating and a little out of breath, she pulled in from the shore and onto the softer sand, her wet feet collecting it and kicking up in her wake. As she gained on her neighbour's house, she could see someone she didn't recognise struggling with a sunbed.

"Hey, need a hand?" she called out. The woman turned towards the voice, her hand raised to shield her eyes from the low setting sun. Dark hair blew around her face in the breeze. She was tanned, covered in tattoos, and Cam was pretty sure she had just been given the once-over. She shrugged it off and held out her hand. "Cam Thomas, I live just a couple of doors down."

"Serena Parker, I'm just staying here while Quinn is away."

"Oh, Quinn's away? Good for her, somewhere nice I hope," she said, lifting the sunbed and pulling out the part that Serena hadn't worked out.

"I dunno, she just asked if I would look after the place for a while," Serena answered, twirling her finger in her hair. "I am hoping to enjoy my time here." She stood back, one arm wrapped around her waist while the other hand continued to twirl her hair. Her weight was placed on one foot. She gazed intently at Cam before her eyes moved to the tall woman standing back and to the side. Carrie kept her eyes firmly on the new neighbour until she was sure she was no threat.

"Well, there ya go." Cam laid the bed out as it should be. "That should work now."

"Thanks, feel free to come over anytime." Serena winked. "I'm sure I can find some way to thank you."

"Oh, well I uh..." She looked up and saw Michelle standing on the veranda, looking her way. "I need to get going, nice to meet you." Jogging the short distance to her own home, she could see Michelle smiling at her as she climbed the steps up to the veranda. "Hey, you."

"Hi, making new friends?" Michelle grinned, pressing her lips against their match. "She looks nice." She smiled, kissing her again before she teased, "Just your type."

"Oh, very funny." Cam laughed and grabbed her wife around the waist. "Let me get showered and I'll show you just who my type is."

"Mm, how about I just join you?"

~Yes~

Naked and in bed with her wife was pretty much the only place Cam wanted to be right now. Dinner plans had gone out of the window the second the shower had been switched on and the room filled with steam. Cam pulled off her running gear like a woman possessed before she climbed in under the water. Her eyes never left the sight of Michelle as she worked slowly to strip out of her own clothing, teasing and tantalising with every move she made. Cam's arousal shot through the roof.

Finally naked, Michelle sauntered into the double shower and wrapped herself around the now wet and aroused body of her wife. "Just a little reminder that I am the only one you need to be admiring."

"Babe, if you think for one second that I am going to look elsewhere, when I get to come home to you, you are so wide of the mark."

Chapter Thirty

OUT should have been silent as she pushed open the door. It was 10 am on a Thursday morning and usually, there wouldn't be anyone here yet. But, right now all she could hear were instruments. Drums banging loudly, guitars riffing, and a microphone screeching as Erin squatted down and fiddled with an amp.

"Well, that didn't take you long!" Cam shouted above the noise. Erin looked up and grinned.

"You said get a band, I got a band!" she replied, sweeping her arm around at the group of people standing around on the stage. The noise had dulled once they realised someone else was in the room.

"I'm glad, let me know when you're gonna be ready to perform and I'll get some publicity going."

"Thanks, Cam...So, this is Trey." She pointed to the guy on guitar, a tall, skinny black guy whose trousers could have been painted on him. He waved a quick hello and went back to studying his string tensions. "Jingo on bass," she added. Jingo was short and chunkier around the middle, his mop of ginger hair hanging loosely around his shoulders. Cam was reminded of a Roald Dahl book she had read as a kid, *The Fantastic Mr Fox,* and its characters Farmer Bunce and Farmer Bean. Holding back a chuckle, she concentrated on Erin, who was still speaking. "And on drums, Serena." Cam looked back towards the large instruments and found the same dark-haired, tattooed woman that was now staying at her neighbour's house.

"Hey," Serena said, waving a hand that held two drumsticks. "I didn't know you worked here too."

Cam smiled. "Yeah, well ya know...gotta pay the bills." She winked at Erin, her manager holding back a giggle. "Anyway, I'll leave you all to it, I need to get upstairs and do some paperwork." She waved a file she was carrying in the air. "Tell Gavin I want a word when he gets here."

~Yes~

A full forty-five minutes later, there was a quiet knock on her office door. It opened slowly to reveal the blonde head of Gavin. He grinned shyly and when she acknowledged him, he pushed the door open fully and entered the room.

"You wanted to see me?"

Cam found herself suddenly nervous. "I did, grab a seat."

He took the nearest seat to the door, long legs stretched out, as relaxed as he had ever looked in front of her. She studied him quickly. She hadn't really noticed it before, just how alike they were. She was a little blonder than him, but only because she had highlights put in every now and then. They were the same height, give or take an inch or two. Blue eyes. Slim build. He really could be her brother, if she had one.

He sat up straight when he realised she was taking more of an interest in him than usual. "So..." He coughed to clear his throat. "What's up?"

She licked her lips, her mouth suddenly dry. "Okay, I'm just gonna say it, but I want you to know first, that if it's not something you're comfortable with then-"

"Cam," he said, sitting forward in his chair. "Just ask."

She nodded, feeling her cheeks heat and redden. "Alright, Michelle wants a baby." The words spouted from her mouth before she could chicken out. "And the thing is, we need-"

"Yeah, I get it...and you want me to help with that?" His eyes narrowed as he spoke. He looked a little perplexed about it.

"We do." She took a steadying breath. "I realise that it's quite a lot to take in, and maybe you should take some time to think about it."

He shook his head. "No, it's not that...I'm just, you want *me*?" he clarified, confusion still etching his face.

"We talked about it, and you were the first and only person we wanted. We look similar for a start and, well...you're a good man, Gavin. Loyal, intelligent, strong. I'd be proud to have any child that turned out like you." she said, her honest appraisal bringing a wetness to his eyes.

"You think that about me?"

Cam was a little shocked that he seemed to doubt himself so much. "Yeah, I do...we do," she confirmed. "We want to have a child. A child that would be ours, not yours. A child that we would love with everything we have."

"I know that, I'd never doubt that you could be the best parents." He stood up and rubbed the back of his neck as he moved around the room. When he turned back to her, his eyes were misted again. "The thing is, I never thought being a father would happen for me. I was a career soldier and meeting a woman to settle down with had never worked out." He sat back down again and leaned forward. "I'm not sure I could ignore the fact that I have a child. Regardless of how great you and Michelle are, I would still know that there was a life that existed because of me. I don't think I could ignore that. I don't think I could see them every day and not want to love them."

"And that's why we wouldn't ask you to do that." She stood now and moved around the desk, perching her butt on the edge. "Don't get me wrong, we're not going to ask you for permission to make decisions about them, we will be their parents." She wanted to make that clear to him from the get-go. "But we'd never stop them from knowing you as their father. You'd be a part of their life."

"Can I take a couple of days to think about it?"

"Of course, we're not in any rush. I mean, we're just putting things in place for when we're ready, so take ya time." She grabbed her keys and stood. "I'm going to head home," she added quickly when he went to stand and follow her out.

"Okay, well I have work to do here," he said, standing anyway. "Next week's rota needs re-organising." He stopped Cam with a touch of the arm. "I will give it serious thought."

"I know you will."

~Yes~

Downstairs, Erin and her band were actually playing something Cam knew. She snuck down the staircase and listened in. It was good, a little rusty as they needed time to adjust to each other and practice, but Cam was pretty pleased with herself that she had overheard Erin that afternoon. This was going to be a big hit, she could feel it.

The music came to a crashing end. A crescendo of drums and guitar played out the last notes with Erin's head bouncing up and down along with the beat, until finally there was silence, and then whoops and high fives all around.

Cam applauded as she came out from behind the bar. "That was awesome!" she exclaimed with a huge grin. Erin jumped down from the small stage area and hugged her, exuberance and adrenaline flowing through her system still.

"Ya know, I thought you were crazy when you suggested this, but now, I dunno...I think it might work." She grinned and acknowledged the other members of her new band.

"So, you got a name yet?" Cam asked.

"Nah, nothing yet. This is the first time we really had the chance to jam. Serena only got the gig last night." Serena looked up at the mention of her name. She raised her arms and lifted her hair to allow some air to the back of her neck. She stood then and moved off the stage to stand within earshot.

"Great, well listen, I am going to get going, but I'll be back in tonight."

"You heading back to the beach?" Serena asked Cam as she pulled a loose-fitting jumper over her skimpy vest, covering the image of a woman and child that had been permanently inked into the skin of her bicep. Cam was intrigued with the designs. Roses and skulls, chains and a couple of butterflies all intertwined together to make a sleeve.

"I am, need a lift?"

"If you don't mind, I just need to grab my bag." She smiled and held Cam's gaze.

"Fine, I'll be outside in the car." Cam nodded to Erin and then left. Her car and Erin's were the only vehicles in the lot. The shiny BMW that Michelle had given her was still gleaming, Erin's pride and joy. Cam chuckled to herself as she climbed into the Ferrari and waited.

When Serena sauntered outside, she raised her hand to guard her eyes against the sunlight. The skirt she wore was what

Pippa Thomas would call "slutty." Cam called it daring. Serena was, in anyone's opinion, hot. She had that look about her that couldn't go unnoticed, and Cam imagined there would be a lot of interest in her from the clients of OUT.

The new drummer put one foot in front of the other and began walking, with confidence, towards the car. Cam could see Erin watching Serena from behind, appreciation on her face as she enjoyed the view. Serena was oblivious to it, and that made Cam smile to herself.

A wall of dark hair placed a shadow over the side window as Serena bent down to look inside the Ferrari. Cam smiled at her this time as she opened the door, folding herself into the passenger seat.

"Thanks for this," Serena said, reaching for the seatbelt. "It's a real pain with my car in the shop."

"Nothing serious, I hope," Cam said, as she slipped the car into gear and pulled away. It glided across the asphalt with a throaty roar.

"No idea, it's a car. I can drive it, but that's about all I know." She grinned, twisting in her seat to face Cam. "Although, if I drove something like this, I might take more of an interest." Her voice lowered several octaves as her eyes glided over Cam's profile, her tongue licking her lower lip. "You don't just work in the bar, do you?"

Cam laughed and shook her head. "No."

Chapter Thirty-One

Michelle heard the sound of the engine before the car pulled up and she hurried to the door to meet Cam, eager to hear all about her discussion with Gavin. She hadn't expected to see the neighbour's house sitter step out from the passenger side of the car and linger as though she had a reason to. Her fingertips skimmed the paintwork delicately as though the car were a living, breathing thing. She took a slow amble around the front of the vehicle, her eyes never leaving Camryn. It spiked a hint of interest in Michelle as she watched the scene play out. Cam hadn't even glanced at her yet, and Michelle bit her lip as she waited to see the outcome of Lil Miss Slutty's display.

When Cam finally looked up from whatever it was she was doing in the footwell, she found that the tattooed hottie had perched her butt on the hood of the car, her really expensive and highly polished car. The door opened and Cam stepped out, pulling her aviators from her eyes to glare a little. It must have worked because the woman instantly stood, but then she stepped up and leaned in to kiss Cam on the cheek.

Michelle glared, ready to go out there and lay claim to her wife once and for all. But she held back and waited for Cam to react first.

"Thanks for the ride," Serena said, breathlessly as though the spirit of Marilyn Monroe had invaded her soul.

"Sure," Cam looked over towards where she could feel eyes on her, eyes she wanted on her always. She grinned at Michelle. "If you'll excuse me, I need to see my wife."

Serena looked across at Michelle too, a thin smile on her lips. "Oh, sure, of course." Serena took a step backwards but kept her eyes firmly on Camryn. "I'll see you around then."

There was no reply from Cam, as she was already moving towards the house and Michelle. "Hey gorgeous, miss me?" she beamed.

"I might have done...new friend getting rides now?" she said it with a smile, but there was an edge to her voice that Cam had only heard once before: back in Greece when jealous Michelle had reared her head, making her claim on Camryn clear. She had been upset about Sarah. Cam couldn't even remember her, but Michelle did. She was doing a good job of controlling the emotion, but it was there under the surface, and Cam was aware.

Michelle stepped away from the door to allow Cam entrance, keeping Serena in her sights. "She's drumming in Erin's new band. It didn't hurt to give her a lift." Cam shrugged and leant in for a kiss as Michelle shut the door.

"Just a ride?" Her brow arched.

Cam smirked. She moved forward, grasping a hold of her wife's hips. "Green looks good on you when you wear a dress...but you don't need to wear it on your skin." She nipped at Michelle's lips, gently nudging her backwards until her back was flush with the wall. "I don't ever want you to think I would ever look anywhere but right here." Cam's palms moved, skimming over Michelle's blouse and across her breasts before moving upwards until she held her face in her palms. "I love you, I'm not looking for anyone else to fulfil anything for me that I am not already getting here, with you."

"I can't help it, I saw the way she looked at you."

"And I see the way people look at you, but I know whose bed you'll be sleeping in. I know who you'll be making love to." Cam held her gaze, forcing her to see the truth within her eyes. "I'm not interested in anyone else. Serena could throw herself naked at me and I'd pass her a robe. It's you, Michelle, always has been."

"I know, rationally, I know that!" She felt stupid. Not once had she ever felt jealousy for anyone she dated. Not once. Her eyes closed as she tried to compose herself. "I've never had anyone to lose before." She shook her head. "I'm sorry, I'm being ridiculous." She laughed at herself. "Come on, Maria left us dinner and I want to hear all about the talk with Gavin.

~Yes~

A simple dish of chicken birria was the meal they would share. The small table outside on the veranda was still bathed in sunlight. Cam gazed out over the ocean and basked in it all for a moment. She could hear the seagulls calling to one another behind the backdrop of crashing waves. It was relaxing and just where she wanted to be right now.

"So, you spoke to Gavin?" Michelle asked as she placed two bowls of steaming goodness down on the table. Cam had opened a bottle of sparkling water and poured two glasses. She took a sip from hers. Her phone lit up and buzzed against the table as it rang. As she reached for it, it cut off. She shrugged at the lack of a name or number to return the call.

"I did." She looked up and held Michelle's hopeful gaze. "He wants to think about it."

"Understandable," she replied, raising her spoon to her lips and blowing gently on the hot stew. "Did you get the impression that he might-"

"I got the impression that he was a little overwhelmed but delighted that we would consider him above all others."

Michelle let out a breath. "Okay, sorry, I'm just so excited about the whole thing, ya know?"

Cam leant across and kissed her. "Yes, I feel the same way. But whatever happens with Gavin, we will find a way to do this that works for us, when we are ready to do it."

Chapter Thirty-Two

The Audi was a comfortable drive as Cam pushed it through the Friday afternoon traffic. It glided imperceptibly around corners and drifted easily between lanes when another car came into view to overtake.

She had arrived at the studio to collect Michelle at one. Filming had run over by an hour and by the time Michelle was finally ready, Cam was itching to get moving. It was a long drive ahead and in hindsight, a flight would have been a better option, but Cam loved to drive these roads. Once they got out of LA and onto the highways that would lead them north, the traffic would thin out and the air con would keep them cool. Several stops at Starbucks along the way would ensure a caffeinated Camryn Thomas would happily keep on moving.

Michelle hit the play button on the stereo and soft music filled the space around them. Cam often listened to classical music when she drove or was at work in her office. It soothed her and kept her calm. Michelle sat back in her seat, tilting it backwards a little, and got comfortable. She felt the warmth of Cam's palm rest easily on her thigh and she sighed. She was as content as she could be with the world outside passing them by in a blur.

She had been on set since just after 4 a.m. and was just about managing to keep her eyes open now. The rhythmic movement of Cam's palm sliding up and down her leg was soothing, and the gentle sway of the vehicle as it gained speed was lulling her to sleep.

"Babe, time to wake up." Cam's voice filtered through and disturbed her dream. "Chelle, you have to wake up sweetheart."

"Hmm, where are we?" she answered, sleepy and docile still. Her eyes fluttered open and found ice blue staring back at her. Her favourite view. "Hi."

Camryn grinned at her as she rubbed the sleep from her eyes. "Hi, hungry?"

"Famished, where are we?" She repeated the question as she looked around at their surroundings.

"No idea, I just pulled off the highway cos I saw the sign for Denny's." Cam continued to smile and pointed out of the window at the building in front of them. It wasn't quite dark yet, but the night was definitely closing in. "We're not far though."

"You must be tired, what time is it?" She unbuckled her seatbelt and stretched out as much as she could.

"Nearly seven. Don't tell anyone, but I put my foot down." Cam grinned and opened the door, climbed out and stretched her own limbs before walking around the vehicle to meet Michelle. Breaking the speed limit here and there had shaved probably an hour off the journey time.

"Let's just grab burgers and get going again. I want to climb into bed with you and snuggle," Michelle said, linking arms with her wife as they walked towards the restaurant.

"I have no arguments with that!"

~Yes~

Cam pulled the car off the main road and down a quiet track. The road was bumpy and she was glad she had driven the Audi and not the Ferrari for this trip.

"Is this it?" Michelle asked, looking out into the darkness. The road was getting narrower as trees and bushes encroached. The headlights lit up the path ahead, sweeping up and down as the car bumped its way along.

"I think so, it's hard to tell," Cam replied. They both looked around, trying to spot the cabin. Just as suddenly as the tarmac had disappeared, it was back again. The cabin loomed up from the darkness as the headlamps picked it out.

"Oh, isn't it cute!"

"Yeah," Cam agreed as she pulled the car into a parking space right outside and jumped out. "Let's get inside then. Kettle on and a nice cuppa before hitting the sack. Then in the morning we can go out and explore." She lifted a stone statue and picked up a shiny key, tossing it to Michelle. "I'll grab the bags."

She dropped the holdalls on the floor in the hallway and looked around. She probably wouldn't describe this house as a cabin, because it was much more than that. It had two floors for a start. In Cam's mind a cabin was nothing more than a small wooden shack in the woods with a couple of rooms and a wood stove. This was kind of like that – it was made of wood and surrounded by trees it was much grander. The entire lower floor was open plan, with a large kitchen area with a nice-sized island that separated it from the living area. There were two doors to the left side of the room. One led to a large utility area; the other was a wet room.

"Cam, this is amazing!"

"I know, right? I was just kind of being nosey on GoodMoves, ya know the house sales site?"

Michelle nodded, an eyebrow raised as to why Cam was being nosey on a house sale site.

"I just like looking at the houses." Cam grinned in response. "Anyway, I saw this place and I was thinking how nice it would be to just get away from it all…it's a new build, and there are only three other cabins along this part of the lake." She yawned before continuing. "And the town is quite small really, one of those quaint little places where everyone knows each other."

"Sounds nice." Michelle handed over a cup of hot tea, and Cam took it from her with a grateful smile.

"I gave the realtor a call and they suggested a trial run, so here we are. We can stay till Tuesday and then I said I'd let them know if we're going to make an offer."

"Well, I am looking forward to exploring tomorrow, but right now, I need to sleep!"

Chapter Thirty-Three

King's Beach on Lake Tahoe was a beautiful spot. Cam stood outside of the cabin, mug of coffee between her palms as her fingers wrapped around the cup, looking across the lake. In the daylight, she could now see that there was another route she could have taken. A long line of black tarmac wiggled its way along the bottom of the drive in both directions. It wound its way around the lake before diverting off and up into the trees further along. Her neighbours were evenly spaced out, one set back a little further than this cabin, while the other looked much closer to the water. She watched as early rowers took advantage of the calm water. Only once had Cam rowed a boat, back when Kate and herself had taken a trip on the train and ended up in Richmond. They hired a small row boat and set off along the Thames. It had been fun, once they had worked out how the oars worked.

Warm arms snaked around her waist as Michelle found a comfortable shoulder to rest her chin on. "God, that shower is just amazing. We need one at home."

"Yeah, I thought that too." Cam smiled, thinking back to the rain shower she had taken that morning. The designers clearly loved their gadgets. Not only was the shower like a rainfall, but they had speakers inside that played nature sounds and the lighting was colour-changing. It was like being naked under a waterfall in the middle of paradise.

Michelle slid her palms lower and into the pockets of Cam's cargo pants. "So, what do you have planned for today?"

"Nothing much, that's the point. But, we do need to find a store and get some food in."

"Okay, how far away is it?"

Cam shrugged, "I think we passed one on the way in last night, but it was too dark to really pay much attention."

"Well, may as well have an adventure and find it."

~Yes~

Rita's Store was a good size, considering how small the town was. Michelle assumed that Rita must get quite a lot of local business around here, and a visit here was probably the highlight of the day for social interaction.

She followed Camryn inside and waited while Cam pulled a small cart from the line. A family stood together near the till. The tall blonde woman with her back to them had a cap on her head. It was pulled down low to hide a scar, but the scar was visible as she turned to see who had entered the store, and Michelle was pretty sure she heard the slight lilt of an English accent as she spoke to a woman she could only assume was Rita. An older woman with a welcoming face smiled at them both. There was another woman in the group, tall like herself, dark-haired like herself too. Only, where Michelle had confidence and held her head high, this woman seemed a little unsure of herself. It was the kids that noticed Michelle first. Two little ones were whispering to one another conspiratorially. They glanced up at her, barely paying any attention before they then leaned in over the baby in the pushchair, he or she giggling at them. But, the older child was wide-eyed as she fixed her intense gaze on Michelle.

"Okay, so the essentials? Milk, bread, cheese, wine..." Cam laughed as she turned with the trolley, ready to saunter down the aisle, completely oblivious to it all.

"Shelly Hamlin?" the young girl whispered to herself, but Michelle heard her. She smiled at her with a wink, and the little one blushed before turning to the woman in the cap and urgently tugging at her sleeve.

Michelle was intrigued as she watched what was clearly a family interact with one another. The blonde woman stopped speaking to Rita and turned to face the young girl. Dropping down to her level, she smiled. "What's the matter?"

The little girl, who was the image of the other woman with her dark curls and big brown eyes, leaned in, cupping her hand around her mouth as she whispered something into the woman's ear that meant she had to turn a little more to look up at Michelle. She too then blushed slightly before she straightened up.

"Hello." Michelle waved with a smile towards the group. Cam stopped fidgeting with the trolley and looked around to see who Michelle was speaking to.

"It's you, isn't it?" the young girl said, her voice filled with hope and awe.

Michelle nodded. "It is, but shhh." She placed her finger to her lips and then, like the other woman before her did, she too dropped down to the child's level. "Cam and I are hoping for a nice, quiet vacation."

"Your secret is safe with me."

"Phew, that's great." Michelle smiled, looking up at the three women all now staring down at her. She noticed that the blonde woman kept her head turned slightly away, but not before she confirmed the long scar that streaked down her cheek. Michelle turned back to the girl. "What's your name?"

"Storm."

"Wow, that's a great name," Michelle gushed, her face lighting up at the little girl's reaction to her.

Storm leant forward like she had with the woman. Again, she cupped her hand before she whispered, "You're my favourite. I wanna be just like Andi Stark when I grow up."

"That is a very admirable thing to grow into," she whispered back before she stood up again and smiled at the three women who had now turned their full attention to the fact that a celebrity was in the store with them.

Cam reached around Michelle and held her hand out to the darker-haired woman. "Hey, Cam Thomas. This is my wife Michelle, uh, Shelly Hamlin."

"Oh, Nicole," she replied, a little starstruck as she took the hand offered.

Before Nicole had a chance to speak, Lucy was already stepping forward with her hand out. "Hi, Lucy Owen. I'm Nicole's fiancée and these are our children, Rain and Summer, Wynter there in the pushchair and, you've already met our little star, Storm." She seemed a lot more self-assured than Nicole, even if she was trying to hide the fact that her face was scarred. When Cam looked down at their joined hands, she noticed further scarring there too. There was a small cough from behind. "Oh and this is Rita, she owns the store." Lucy blushed at almost forgetting the older woman.

"Hi." Handshakes followed all around as everyone became acquainted.

"Well, it was lovely to meet you all, but we really need to get moving." Cam smiled as the youngster groaned. "Otherwise we will starve!" she joked.

They moved away and began to grab items from the shelves. Michelle was reminded of a time not so long ago, in Greece, when they were barely on speaking terms. She shook her head at the memory. Things had changed so much for them both. She smiled as she watched Cam take a jar of green olives and place them into the cart.

When they were out of earshot, Michelle nudged her and leant in to speak. "That could be us one day."

Eyes wide, Cam exclaimed, "Four?"

"Well, maybe two."

They were halfway down the aisle when she was aware of small footsteps running down the aisle behind them. She turned and found Storm smiling up at her.

"Hello again." Cam grinned.

"You sound like my Mama," she answered, tilting her head. "You're from England too?"

"I am, is that where your Mama is from?"

Storm nodded proudly. "She used to be famous too."

"Oh, did she?" Cam continued. The kid was kind of cute. "What was she famous for?"

"Oh, she was a singer, in a really famous band," Storm continued. "Solar Flare," she said with as much pride as if she had been in the band herself.

Cam stopped grinning and looked back to the woman herself as she limped towards them. "Storm, come on, stop bothering the ladies." She looked a little nervous as she realised that Camryn was staring at her.

"You, you're...Lucy Owen?" Cam stuttered, much to Michelle's amusement.

"Uh, yeah...I just told you that." She thumbed over her shoulder back toward where they had all stood moments earlier.

"Yes, yes of course, but I mean... *the* Lucy Owen?" Cam tried again, realising she wasn't quite making much sense. "From Solar Flare?"

Lucy nodded, her cheeks blushing. "You're a fan?"

Cam nodded. "Yeah, I had all your records."

Chapter Thirty-Four

"Lucy Owen! How did I not see that coming?" Cam said as she unloaded their shopping bags into the fridge and cupboards. Michelle was touching up her make-up and watching Cam through the mirror above the fireplace. It was moments like this that Michelle loved most, just the two of them talking about insignificant things. Normal everyday couple stuff that the newspapers couldn't write about.

"They were like one of the biggest bands around," Cam insisted before adding, "She was hot!"

"Oh really?" Michelle swung around to glare at Cam, who right now was just realising exactly what she had said, attempting to backtrack instantly.

"Well, yeah. I mean, ya know." Squirming at the attention that comment had gotten her, she blushed terribly. "Back in the day...Sorry."

Michelle grinned. "Honey I am kidding, I am not jealous of your schoolgirl crushes."

Relieved, Cam tossed a small towel at her. "You are horrible." She laughed. The smile slowly slid from her face as a memory invaded her mind. "Such a shame what happened really, they were going to be a huge hit around the world," she continued, gushing about Lucy.

"What happened?" Michelle asked, sincerely interested in Lucy's story.

Cam watched Michelle as she turned towards her, head tilted as she pushed a stud into her lobe. "They were involved in an accident," Cam explained, her eyes still following as Michelle crossed the room to where Cam perched on the edge of the couch. One leg raised and then the other until she was straddling Cam's lap.

"Hi," Cam said, when Michelle was settled. Her mind was now going elsewhere, palms sliding easily along bare thighs.

"Hi," Michelle returned. "So, go on," she implored as she felt Cam's fingers tease knowingly, higher to cup her behind, closing off any space between them.

"Well, if I remember correctly they had just come off stage and were on their tour bus heading for the airport when it crashed." Michelle had cupped her face and was stroking her cheek. "Several of the band were killed and Lucy was in hospital for a long time."

"Oh my God. How awful, ya know I think I remember reading about that, now that you mention it."

"Yeah, I can't even imagine how bad that must have been. It was huge news in the UK."

"Oh sweetie, you must have been distraught," Michelle said, with a mischievous look in her eye. "Ya know, when your crush just disappeared."

"Really? You're gonna go there?" Cam smiled up at her and pulled her in a little tighter to her lap.

"Oh, I am so going to go there. So, did you kiss your poster goodnight?" she laughed.

"Uh huh, yep I did. I might even go over there right now and admit my undying love." She laughed along with her wife.

"Ha, well why don't I show you just why it is that you should stay right here, with me? Your *new* crush," Michelle said, pushing Cam down with her palms against her shoulders until she was lying prone on her back, trapped by her thighs. "I think you'll find that I am well worth your admiration."

~Yes~

They walked for what felt like miles, skirting the edge of the lake as much as they could until finally they were forced up a small path that led from a jetty up towards a cabin that was hidden behind overgrown shrubbery and looking like it was long forgotten.

Hand in hand they strolled, enjoying the clean air and the greenery.

"This is nice, right?" Cam asked.

Michelle tightened her grip. "It is. I'm glad we came."

"Me too. I know it's only been a day, but I already feel at home here."

The sound of children playing brought their attention to their left as the two little girls from earlier came hurtling towards them in swimming costumes, carrying nets and buckets, squealing with excitement as Nicole gave chase.

"It would be nice to bring our own kids here one day, don't you think?"

"Oh hey," Nicole said, out of breath and smiling. "We uh, we're all just heading down to the lake for some fishing." Cam noticed over her shoulder that Lucy was limping along behind carrying the baby, accompanied by Storm.

"Sounds great," Cam replied as they all came to a halt. "This is where you live?" she asked, looking around as Lucy finally caught up and Storm recognised them again.

"Yes, it's wonderful, don't you think?" Nicole gushed.

Michelle nodded. "It's completely idyllic."

"We're thinking of buying a place so we can get away from it all now and then," Cam added as Lucy and Storm caught up.

"Are you going to live here?!" Storm gushed, her eyes lighting up at the prospect of Shelly Hamlin living nearby.

"Well, our home will be in LA, for now. But, it would be nice to have somewhere to visit when we need a break."

"Wow," Storm said. "You should come to dinner. Mama is making a huge lasagne, it's my favourite."

"Oh, I am sure that would be lovely, but your mom's..."

Nicole cut Michelle off quickly. "We would love to have you over, I mean, if you're not busy of course."

Cam grinned, turning to Michelle for an answer. "Okay, well, if you're sure."

"Yes!" Storm jumped up excitedly, her quick movement scaring the baby, who promptly burst into tears. "Sorry." She forgot all about her famous idol and instantly stuck her face towards the baby to pacify him. When he wouldn't stop, Nicole called over one of the younger girls, Rain.

"Work your magic, kiddo." Lucy laughed as the youngster ran over and skidded to a halt.

"Hey Wyn, why are you crying? Did you want to come and find some fish?" Instantly the little boy began to quieten down, his big brown eyes staring up at his older sister as she spoke to him.

"All through my pregnancy, he always reacted to Rain's voice." Nicole smiled, proudly looking on at her family.

"That's so cute," Cam said. Once the baby was settled, Rain tugged on Nicole's sleeve and began pulling her to the lake.

"I guess we had better let you get going." Michelle laughed at the youngster's antics.

"Yeah, or we will never hear the end of it. So, uh dinner...please don't feel obligated, but we would be happy to have you both come over, say 7?" Lucy smiled, offering them a way out.

"Seven will be great," Michelle answered for them both. "So, can we get back into town this way?" she asked, pointing up the pathway.

Lucy smiled, and Cam watched the scar that zagged across her left cheek crinkle. "Yep, right to the top and turn left, then it's about a 20-minute walk."

~Yes~

At the back of the cabin a small dock had been built. Attached to that was a small rowing boat that could be used to row out to a floating deck. It was only twenty or thirty feet out, and Michelle planned to swim out to it and enjoy a little sunbathing with Cam. There were other people out and about in boats of all sizes, but the area around the cabin was still pretty secluded.

Wandering out from the cabin in just her swimsuit, Cam whistled. "It's a good job we're not in Antarctica!" She paused and waited for Michelle to reply. Instead, the actress just stood, hand on hip and waiting for the inevitable joke.

One eyebrow raised, she finally replied. "Why?"

Cam sniggered. "Because, you're so hot, it would melt." She watched as Michelle tried not to react, but the corners of her mouth were threatening it. "Oh, come on, that was funny!"

Michelle walked towards her, now openly smiling. "No, it was awful, but I appreciate the compliment!" She grabbed hold of Cam's collar and kissed her. When she was done, she stepped back and smoothed out her shirt. "When are you getting changed?"

"For?"

"A swim?" Her eyes were boring into Cam's, Lust evident still.

"Ah, I wasn't planning to swim," Cam said, looking around them at all the people out on the lake. "I have this book I was going to read."

Michelle raised a brow again. "Seriously, you're turning all this," she swept her hands down her own body, "down so you can read a book?" She said the last four words as slowly as she could so that Cam had time to process that statement.

"Well..." Cam sucked in a breath and bit her lip as she breathed out. "We could just skip the swimming and go inside?"

Michelle studied her, her eyes narrowing as she noticed the subtle squirm Camryn reacted with when she finished speaking.

"You're doing it again," Michelle said quietly, reaching out for her and tugging her close again. "You're hiding from me."

Cam shook her head. "No, I'm not." Her words said one thing, but the blush that covered her neck and cheeks said otherwise.

Michelle's head tilted as she watched her avoid the truth, her memory taking her back to the times that Cam wouldn't even think about taking her clothes off. She almost grinned at the memory of OUT's parking lot, when they had not been together and Cam was making a point to Erin by stripping out of her bike leathers and changing into her clothes in front of a full cast and crew of *Medical Diaries*, who were filming that day. "Camryn?"

"Fine, it's not you. I just don't want to be on show to all these people." She swept out her hand towards the handful of human beings scattered in various boats around the expanse of water.

"Because?"

Cam huffed. "Because you know why."

Michelle's voice softened. "Camryn, nobody is looking at us, and to honest Babe, if they do, it's probably me that they will stare at." She smiled; the perils of being on TV and the movies meant rarely was anywhere private. "And, so what if they look at your scars? All they prove is how brave you are." Cam still looked unconvinced. "Look, why don't you get changed and wear a t-shirt while you row out to the dock and then, if you still feel uncomfortable, I won't push you?"

Cam looked out at the water. The nearest boater was probably 500 feet away. She nodded. "Alright."

Chapter Thirty-Five

The taxi arrived on time and dropped them off at the top of the road that led down to Lucy and Nicole's cabin. They could have walked the entire journey, but without really knowing the area, Michelle didn't want to risk getting lost. It was almost dark, but still quite warm this time of the year, edging towards the end of May. Cam thought this place would be amazing in the autumn.

"Do you think we should have brought a better gift?" Cam asked, suddenly struck with nerves.

Michelle stopped in her tracks and looked at her. "Oh my God," she laughed, "You still think she's hot, don't you?"

"No, of course not." Cam tried to appear nonchalant. "I just... is a bottle of wine enough, I mean...I haven't been invited to someone's house like this for years."

"*And* you think she's hot." Michelle continued to tease as they started to walk again.

"I do not, stop saying that," Cam argued, her cheeks blushing. "Of course, she's an attractive woman, they both are, but that's not..."

"Oh, you think they're both hot. Okay, I get it." Michelle laughed and turned quickly, bumping against Cam's midriff. "It's okay baby, I don't mind, just so long as I'm the one you come home with." She winked, then leaned forward and kissed Cam's mouth, before turning and walking off, leaving the blonde in shock at her antics.

Finally getting herself together, Cam shouted, "Very funny, next time we're out and that woman you like is around, I am going to have *so* much fun."

Michelle came to a halt and tilted her head. "What woman?"

"What woman?" Cam tutted. "You know what woman, the one that organises your locations department." Michelle instantly blushed. "Yeah, that woman. Anna, isn't it? I've seen how you get all giddy when she turns up."

They both burst into laughter as they reached the door. "It's a very expensive bottle, I am sure it will be fine and anyway, it's not like there was much to choose from at Rita's."

The door opened before they even had time to knock or get themselves together. Storm stood in the doorway smiling at them and wondering why they were laughing so much.

~Yes~

Trying to get Storm to go to bed that evening was an event in itself. Dinner had been fun, lots of conversations and getting to know one another. Both couples found they had quite a lot in common, which made it much easier to entertain one another. Storm, though, was in awe. For the first 15 minutes she did nothing but stare at Michelle.

This was her idol, sitting in her own living room, on her couch, next to her. Realising the effect she was having on the young girl, Michelle went out of her way to initiate conversation, and finally the youngster had found her words. And boy did she have questions.

Lucy and Nicole apologised several times, but Michelle had waved them off. She was fine with it and was impressed with Storm's knowledge of the show she had been in previously.

"Storm, it's way past your bedtime now," Nicole warned. She had been trying for the past thirty minutes to get her daughter into bed. The kid had used every excuse to get up and come back out. She needed a drink...then the toilet...then another drink...then she heard a noise.

"How about I come and sit with you while you go to sleep?" Michelle offered. The youngster was yawning and could barely keep her eyes open. It really wouldn't be much longer before she was sleeping soundly.

Storm nodded and looked to her mother for approval. "You don't mind?" Nicole asked Michelle. "I don't see her settling anytime soon otherwise."

Michelle smiled and held out her hand for Storm. "Come on, getting a good night's sleep is one of the most important things you can do."

"Really?" Storm asked, rubbing at her eyes.

"Yes." She nodded. "How else would I remember all my lines if I were tired all the time?" Michelle continued as they crossed the room towards Storm's room.

"I guess so," Storm was heard replying as they entered the room.

"She's really good with the kids," Lucy said to Cam, jutting her chin towards Michelle.

Cam was still staring at the bedroom door. "Yeah, she is," she agreed.

"You thought about it?"

"About?" Cam inquired, turning to face Lucy.

"Having kids. You both seem so natural with them."

"Oh." Usually Cam would be a little more reticent at telling virtual strangers about their plans, but with Lucy and Nicole, she was already beginning to feel comfortable. It felt as though they were all old friends. "We've discussed it, yeah."

"But not come to a conclusion?"

"Well, Michelle really wants to have a baby..."

"And you're not so sure?" Lucy asked. She moved and grimaced as she tugged her leg up onto the couch to stretch it out.

Cam shrugged. "I do want them, I just dunno if now is the right time."

Lucy nodded sagely. "Until I met Nicole, I never thought I wanted them...it didn't even enter my head that I'd ever be in a relationship again, never mind have the opportunity to be a parent." She smiled over at Nicole as the brunette stood. "I wouldn't change my life for the world. Being a parent, it's just the best feeling ever." Nicole squeezed her shoulder as she passed on her way to make some more coffee in the kitchen.

"I don't doubt it." Cam answered. "I just...Is it too soon, ya know? Everything has happened so fast, we met, fell in love and got married all within the space of a few months, and then there's the whole..." She wondered how much of their life these women knew about. "I'm still coming to terms with a lot of stuff after...Jessica."

"She was the woman in the news? The one that attacked you?" Lucy probed. Storm had mentioned the story anytime she was at Rita's and caught a headline in one of the tabloids or gossip magazines.

"Yeah. Physically I'm doing well. But I still have some issues with the...Uh..." She was a little embarrassed about it, especially looking into the face of a woman who was scarred herself. Maybe Lucy would understand. "How do you...ya know with the scar, how do you deal with that?"

Lucy smiled. "It took a long time. This isn't the only scar I have." Her finger trailed down her own cheek and she chuckled at Cam's raised brows. "When I was in the bus, when it crashed? I was pretty much dragged along the road with it. I'm sure you've already noticed that I limp?" she said, tugging the leg of her trousers upwards to reveal the scars that marked her leg all the way up to her knee and continued on underneath the material covering her thigh. "My scars are everywhere, so I get it, Cam. You have scars?"

Cam nodded. "I was stabbed, several times. And then, in the hospital they had to..." She reached up and opened the top button on her shirt to reveal the pink line that made its way down her chest.

Lucy whistled. "That's a good one, huh?" She grinned, and Cam couldn't help but grin back. "You can't change it Cam, it is what it is and you can either accept them and own them, or forever hide behind clothes and people. What does Michelle say?"

Nicole came back with a pot of coffee to refresh their cups. Aware that something a little heavier was being discussed, she sat down quietly and began to pour.

"She's great." Cam couldn't keep the grin from her face when she looked up and saw her wife tiptoeing out of Storm's room. "She loves me regardless, but I don't want to be the kind of parent that's fucked up."

Unsure what they were talking about, Michelle tilted her head at her wife's frowning face. "All okay?"

"Yeah, just talking scars with Lucy," Cam answered, reaching a hand out to tug her wife gently back into the seat beside her. "Storm asleep now?"

"Yes, she fought it as best she could." Michelle giggled.

"You're gonna be such a good mum." The sincerity in Cam's voice almost brought tears to Michelle's eyes.

"I hope so."

"I know so," Cam said, kissing the side of her head.

Chapter Thirty-Six

Morning brought with it a new sense of hope for Cam. She had taken on board what Lucy had said and was determined to try and change the way she felt about her physical appearance. She stood outside by the dock and waved as she saw the family of found friends rowing towards them.

The invitation to spend the day together had been a last-minute thought as Michelle was saying her goodbyes to Nicole. Cam realised just how well the two women were getting along, and Lucy was just the person that Cam needed to spend time with right now. The kids were all kneeling at the front of the boat, looking cute in their tiny orange life-jackets as the waved manically at the figure on the shore. Little Wynter sat quietly in his mother's lap as Lucy powerfully manoeuvred the boat through the water.

Storm was ready to jump out of the boat the moment it set against the dock. Laughing, Cam grabbed hold of her to stop her from toppling backwards into the cool water.

"Storm," Lucy warned, "pretty sure the last time you fell in, you promised to be more careful."

"Sorry Mama." A little pout appeared on her lips before she turned back to Cam and grinned. "Hi Cam."

"Hey. I definitely agree that you shouldn't fall into the water." She paused before adding, "Not fully dressed anyway." She giggled and lifted the kid into the air, carrying her down the dock towards where Michelle was waiting, smiling at their antics.

~Yes~

Nicole and Michelle had set up a blanket on the shoreline. Wynter was currently being held by Michelle, who was positively glowing as she grinned down at him, making all the funny noises that adults seemed to think a baby understood. Cam watched them, standing beside Lucy with their feet in the water as the twins splashed about. Storm was reading Michelle's script. She always carried one in her bag and would often read it during quiet moments, especially if she had a difficult medical scene coming up, which she did.

"Mama?" Rain, one of the twins, called out, her little face smiling up at them from the water. Lucy squatted down to her and listened. "Can you take us to the castle?"

Intrigued that there was a castle, Cam now squatted down too. "The Castle?" Lucy inquired with just as much interest.

"Yeah, over there silly." She pointed out towards the floating dock. Summer came to stand beside her sister, nodding at them.

"I'm the princess and I need to get to my castle," she said before spinning around. "Otherwise I'll turn into a pumkin."

"You mean a pumpkin," Lucy pronounced.

"That's what I said, a pumkin."

Cam laughed and earned a glare from the youngster and a smile from Lucy. "Okay then, let's get the boat."

"Nuh-uh. We have to swim out on our magic dolphins."

"Oh I see, and I suppose that I am a magic dolphin?" she asked, smiling at their imaginative minds.

"Yeah, you and Cam," Rain stated.

Lucy stood up and Cam followed. "So, lesson one in parenting, you're gonna be a magic dolphin often, or a magic horse, a magic car, a magic spaceship..." She chuckled. "It's never ending just how magical you can be!" She laughed again before looking down at the girls.

Without another word, Lucy lifted her t-shirt and pulled it off to reveal a black bikini top and all of her scars. Cam found herself drawn to them, staring at them. Sensing this was something that Cam needed to see, Lucy stood still and waited.

"I used to find this part the hardest too," she said softly as Cam looked away. She walked away, back to where Nicole and Michelle were still fawning over Wynter. Folding her shirt neatly, she placed it on the blanket and then stripped out of her shorts. A part of Cam felt guilty now as she looked at the scars Lucy lived with. How could she even begin to feel sorry for herself when this woman had been through so much more.

When Lucy returned to the water, she reached out and touched Cam's arm. "If you're not ready to be a magic dolphin, it's okay. I can fit them both on my back."

Cam shook her head. Looking at Michelle and how happy she was with a baby in her arms and children playing around her, she knew that this was what she wanted too. "No, it's fine. I wanna be a magic dolphin."

When she took off running up the shore towards the house, Michelle looked up, worry etched across her features. She looked towards Lucy, who signalled that it was okay. Her instinct was to run back into the house and find Cam, find out what was wrong and then lock the world out and protect her. But, minutes later Cam came outside again, wearing her bikini. It wasn't the skimpy kind she used to wear. No more thongs and strings; this was a sportier style with shorts, but it was the first time she had worn it outside and with other people around her. Most of her scars were hidden by the sports bra, but there was nothing she could do about the others unless she wore a full body suit.

Michelle held her breath as she watched the woman she loved walk slowly down to the water's edge, her eyes darting back and forth in case anyone new appeared.

When Cam looked up, she found Lucy nodding and smiling. She kept her breathing as even as she could, taking deep breaths and letting them out slowly. She kept telling herself that she was fine, she could do this, she was a magic dolphin. Her breath hitched in panic when Summer looked up and saw her coming, but she felt the tugging of a smile creep onto her lips when both girls started splashing around and singing about magic dolphins.

"Alright?" Lucy said as she approached.

"Yeah,"

"Okay, let's do this. Which princess do ya want?" They both laughed as the girls decided for them, Summer jumping up at Cam while Rain did the same with Lucy. They hoisted them up and then with a wave to the others, they were off.

The water wasn't that deep. For the most part they could walk out until it hit chest height, all of them whooping as the colder water hit their skin. By the time they started swimming they were only feet from the dock. Cam was a little concerned that Summer would slip off her back, but she needn't have worried; the kid had a grip on her swimsuit and was using it as reins.

~Yes~

The fire pit was alight and warming them as they sat around it. Cam and Lucy had insisted on a BBQ and were cooking up a feast of burgers and hotdogs, both of them complaining about the lack of *real* sausages.

Michelle snuggled against Cam's side as they watched the flames now building again following the addition of several small logs. "I am so proud of you," she whispered before kissing her cheek.

"Lucy helped a lot, and of course, I *was* a magic dolphin!"

Michelle chuckled and kissed Cam's shoulder. "You made a fabulous magic dolphin...I can't wait to have kids with you."

"I think it's going to be the best thing we do, make a family together."

Chapter Thirty-Seven

Cam packed the last bag into the back of the car, while Michelle did a last check to make sure they hadn't left anything behind. The weekend couldn't have gone any better. They had fallen in love with the house on the lake, and Cam had already put an offer in on it, a birthday gift to Michelle. When her phone rang, she assumed it would be the realtor coming back to her with an answer to her offer, but it wasn't. She didn't recognise the number at all. She flicked the green spot on the screen and answered it.

"Hello?"

The line crackled for a second before it disconnected.

"Who was that?" Michelle asked, closing the door and locking it behind her. Cam watched her place the key back in its hiding place.

"No idea, it cut off," she replied, continuing to watch Michelle straighten up, smooth out her trousers, and smile.

She shrugged. "Oh well, I'm sure they will call back. Ready to go?"

"Yeah."

"Okay then. Let's hit the road."

They climbed into the car and Cam began to back out of the parking space. As she looked into the rear-view mirror, she grinned. "I think you have a visitor wanting to say goodbye." Michelle turned her head slightly to check the wing mirror.

"So I see." She grinned as Storm's face came into view; she had grown quite fond of the youngster. "Hey Storm," she called out of the window.

"Hi Shelly." She waved and ran towards the car, poking her face through the window to wave at Cam. "Hi Cam."

"Hey." She wiggled her fingers in reply.

"I just wanted to say goodbye and give you this before you go." She grinned and handed over a piece of paper that was rolled up and tied with a small ribbon. "It's just a picture I drew."

Michelle unravelled it to find a kid's drawing of her character, Andi Stark. "Oh wow, Storm that is so sweet. Thank you so much," Michelle gushed. She reached inside her bag and pulled out her keys. Fiddling for a moment, she said, "I want you to have this." She held out a small keyring with the letter M hanging from it.

"Wow, really?" Storm took the gift and held it tightly between her fingers, looking at it like it were the crown jewels. "I'll look after it."

Michelle laughed. "Of course you will, that's why I am giving it to you."

"You're coming back though, right?" Storm asked, all wide-eyed.

Michelle looked at Cam before looking back at the little girl and nodding. "Yes, we're definitely going to come back."

~Yes~

Michelle pulled the car into the space outside of the beach house and sighed. Finally home again. It had been a long drive back, especially when they had gotten held up in the tailback of a crash on the highway. Air con and the coffee and snacks they had picked up barely fifteen minutes earlier had been a godsend.

Cam jumped out of the car and opened the trunk, wasting no time in grabbing their bags and heading into the house. All she wanted to do now was jump in the pool and cool off.

Her phone rang again from where she had left it on the dashboard. Michelle picked it up and stared at the screen. An unknown number. She answered it anyway.

"Hello?" There was silence for a second before a buzzing and crackling filled the airwaves. "Hello, is anyone there?" It unnerved her a little. Another reminder of Jessica.

"lo...*crackle*...Ca...*crackle*...me...*crackle*...line."

"I'm sorry, I can't hear..."

"Ca...*crackle*...I'm com...*crackle*...hear me?"

"I can't..." The phoneline went dead.

"Who was that?" Cam's smiling face appeared in the open doorway of the car.

"No idea, it's your phone. The line was really bad. I think it was a woman though."

"Strange...I've had a few calls lately where nobody is there." She reached in and took the phone, checking the call list. "Unknown number."

"Should we be worried?"

"Nah." Cam scrunched her nose and smiled. "Probably just a wrong number."

Michelle didn't look so sure as she climbed out of the car and walked towards the house, turning back to flip the beeper and alarm the car. She took a quick glance around, happy that she didn't see anything out of the ordinary.

Chapter Thirty-Eight

Cam was lying on the couch watching TV while Michelle sat in the La-Z-Boy, legs swung off over the arm, laughing at the antics on the show. It had been a long couple of days, and Michelle was enjoying a few hours off; not being needed on set was a godsend sometimes. Earlier she had done some interviews and auditioned for a part in a film that Janice was insistent she try out for. It had been fun, but now all she wanted to do was relax with Cam and watch TV. Cam had been just as busy finalising the details of the cabin sale as well as organising promotion for Erin and her new band night.

The doorbell rang, and both of them looked up and then at each other. Michelle had sent Maria home already, so she got up and, laughing over her shoulder, said, "No, don't you move, I'll get it."

"Okay." Cam grinned and reached out for the remote to pause the TV.

Michelle was so used to having Gavin or one of the team around that she didn't think twice about opening the door. Standing on the other side of it was a tall blonde woman, early forties and very well dressed. She had the most beautiful blue eyes, and they bore in to her now. Familiar eyes.

"Good evening, I am so very sorry to bother you but I am looking for Camryn Thomas and I was pointed in this direction." She spoke elegantly. British, but unlike Camryn, her accent was much more pronounced. She sounded the way Michelle assumed royalty did. Michelle stared at the woman, who stood upright like a board, a small bag by her feet. She was wearing a designer suit that could have been, and probably was, made for her. It was then that Michelle realised who she was looking at.

"Caroline, you must be Caroline!" Michelle announced to the woman, moving her hand forward to take the hand that was already proffered.

"Yes, Caroline Thomas, and I believe you must be Michelle? Your photographs certainly do not do you justice. Is Camryn home?"

"Yes, of course. My goodness, where are my manners, please come on in." She stood to the side and held the door as the older version of Camryn walked in, confident and assured.

"Camryn," Michelle called out as she led Caroline through the house to the living room.

"Yes babe? What is it that's so important you're yelling-" Came the reply from Camryn as she sat up and stretched her back out. She abruptly stopped moving as soon as she saw the guest that Michelle now had by her side.

"Hello Camryn," Caroline said, smiling down at her sister.

"Caroline! What? How? I mean, why?" Cam could barely understand how her sister was standing right in front of her in her own home when they hadn't even spoken for the last 12 months at least. In fact, Camryn had barely heard from her sister at all in the last ten years. She was extremely caught up in her work for the government and rarely had time for anything else. Cam had gotten used to not seeing or speaking to her, so it was strange to have her standing in front of her now.

"Well I hoped you might have been pleased to see me, is it not a good time?" Caroline frowned at Cam's reaction, but politeness dictated she should apologise for just turning up. "I know it's short notice and I didn't send word beforehand, but I tried to call several times. Everything was hush hush, you know how it is?" She smiled again, first to her sister and then to Michelle as if they both knew and understood what she meant by that.

"It's fine, we would love to have you," Michelle interjected as she took Caroline's bag from her. "We have plenty of room, your mother is here too, did you know that?"

Caroline turned to Michelle. "Uh, yes I did know that." And then she turned back to Camryn. "Camryn, I came because...,"

Cam stood up, studying her sister properly now. Miss Put-Together-and-Cool-as-a-Cucumber wasn't looking quite so cool. "What is it?"

She smiled weakly. "I just needed to see my little sister." Then she followed Michelle out of the room.

Cam's eyes narrowed as she considered that for a moment. She didn't believe it for a second. There was more to this story, but right now wasn't the time for it.

Chapter Thirty-Nine

The arrival of Camryn's elusive sister had brought a quiet stillness to the house. Cam made the call to her mother to inform her of her prodigal daughter's unexpected visit, and of course, within thirty minutes Pippa had arrived back from town.

"You okay?" Michelle spoke quietly as Cam was making coffees and tea for everyone. The clanking of cups and spoons as she stirred caused concern.

"Yeah, just surprised I guess." She offered a small smile, but Michelle read it.

"You know you can be honest with me, Cam." She watched as her wife placed the cup she was holding down on the worktop before slowly turning to her.

"I think I am a little bit pissed off with her." She sighed. "She walked out of home the minute she could and she never looked back, never once checked to see if I was okay or if I needed her, and then she would appear every now and then like a whirlwind. Just like now! And Mum and Dad would be all 'Caroline this, Caroline that, you should be more like Caroline, have you seen what Caroline was wearing? Why can't you dress more like Caroline?"

"I never meant for that to happen, Camryn." Her sister stood in the doorway, hands clasped in front of her as she took in the image of her younger sibling now: tall and strong, independent and confident in herself. "I didn't think about anyone else apart from myself, it's what I've always done I suppose." She spoke quietly as she walked further in to the kitchen. "Mum wondered where the tea was." She spoke to Michelle now, a veiled request for some time with Cam.

Cam turned back to her task of making coffee. The tea was brewed already but she made a big deal of stirring the pot anyway. It gave her something to do other than having to look at her sister. When it was made and all laid out on a tray, Michelle took it from Cam. "I'll take it, you two need to talk." She pressed a light kiss to the corner of Cam's mouth before turning to Caroline. A brief smile in return was enough of a thank you for Michelle to leave them to it.

The silence was awkward, but Caroline braved it and went first.

"When you were born, I was the happiest child in the world. I had my own perfect little doll to play with and dress up." Caroline was smiling as she spoke. Cam listened. "You really were the most beautiful baby, with that tuft of blonde hair and those blue eyes so like mine." Camryn heard the scraping of a chair against the tiled floor as Caroline pulled it out and took a seat. "As you grew up, the age gap changed the dynamics I suppose. When I was 15 and wanting to go out with my friends, or on dates with boys, I would always have to take you along with me, and I guess in my teenage angst I grew to resent that. I never resented *you!*" She stressed that point. "But I resented our parents for forcing that on me. I was a typical teenager that didn't want her little sister in tow all the time, but at the same time I loved you, only you weren't my little doll anymore and you didn't want to do the things I did."

Camryn was still yet to speak; she had a feeling that she didn't need to, that Caroline needed to say all this and she needed to hear it. So, she took a seat opposite her sister and stared at her. Caroline had aged a little in the time since they had last seen each other, had lost weight too but not to the point where she looked unwell. Her blonde hair had always been a little darker than Cam's, but now it was greying around the edges. At 43 she was still an attractive woman, but she looked tired, as though life had drained her a little.

"By the time you got to 17, I had just finished university. While I was there I was headhunted by MI6. They saw something in me that they could use, and I grabbed at the opportunity." It surprised Cam at how candid Caroline was being; she had no idea she worked for MI6. Caroline had never really spoken about her work, only that it involved the government and being away from home a lot. "I wanted to see the world and be of use." Cam had always assumed it was administrative, or maybe diplomatic. "Obviously it was, it is *still* a very covert and challenging employment and one I am unable to discuss in too much detail, but I want you to understand why I have been maybe a little bit distant."

Cam's face must have registered the surprise she felt. "Are you a spy?"

Caroline smiled at that and shook her head. "No, not quite."

"Not quite? What does that mean?"

"It means that I wasn't there for you when you needed me, and I am sorry for that. I was unavailable and that's as much as I can tell you, I'm sorry." She smiled ruefully. Her eyes had filled with unshed tears, and she was reaching her hand across the table. "I wish you could forgive me for that, and I hope one day I can explain in more detail, but I can't right now." Cam let her take her hand, and they sat across from one another, holding hands as Caroline continued. "I came home as often as I could and you're right, Mum and Dad made a huge fuss, and I allowed it because, God Cam the things I had seen, I just wanted something normal." She ran her other hand through her hair and left it resting on her head as she sat her elbow on the table. "And then I came home one day and you weren't there, and nobody would explain why or give me a number to contact you. I had to actually ask someone at work to track you down so I could call you, only by then I was sent overseas again and one phone call was all I could manage. But you didn't want to talk about it."

Cam recalled the phone conversation and how she had avoided any talk of their parents or why she wasn't living at home anymore. "I always thought you just couldn't wait to leave," Cam replied quietly. "That getting out was more important than I was to you."

"No, Camryn no, that's just not true. The fact is I chose a career that required not just my time but my silence, and I convinced myself that it was all okay because it was my duty to queen and country, what I do-" She seemed to struggle with what she could and couldn't say. "My job entails secrecy, even with my most trusted loved ones. Lives depend on it!" She let slip as much as she could. She could never give details, never mention the work they undertook to keep the world a safer place.

"Your life?" Cam asked, suddenly aware of what her sister was telling her without saying.

Caroline nodded. "At times, yes. But mostly other people," she quickly added, seeing the fear rise on her little sister's face. "You don't have to worry. That's why I am here. I resigned and have just finished working my notice, tying everything up and passing the reigns to my successor."

"And you came straight here?"

"Yes, I flew in from Hong Kong."

"To see me, or...?"

"To spend time with my family and to get to know them all again, properly." She squeezed Cam's hand. "Thankfully *OK* magazine has pretty much kept me up to date with your life." She chuckled and Cam couldn't help but laugh out loud. Her tone turned more sombre when she added, "I am sorry I couldn't be here when Jessica hurt you. I had someone keeping me informed but it wasn't the same, and if I am honest it was the moment I began to reconsider my career choices and where my life was headed. I wanted to be here with you, meeting your new wife, and yet I was overseas once more, and once again you was left to deal with everything by yourself."

"I didn't expect you to be there."

"But you should have, we all should have been there, Camryn. I know Mum has begun to make amends. I'd like to ask you to maybe give me a second chance too."

Chapter Forty

Michelle climbed into bed bedside Camryn. The blonde was reading the last few chapters of a book she had started months ago and had not had time to just sit and finish. It was a task she was beginning to think would never be accomplished, because her thoughts just couldn't be kept in check, and whether Jack Reacher ever managed to solve this crime in her lifetime was a subject she would have to worry about another day.

She sighed and closed the book, placing it on the bedside cabinet to her left before closing her eyes and releasing a pent-up breath. Her wife sat quietly waiting, knowing she didn't need to ask or push, that Cam would spell it out to her at any moment.

"You wanna talk about it?"

Cam could hear all the sounds of the house as each of the guests finished up their nightly routines and went to bed themselves. The sound of the water system kicking in as Caroline, who was in the room next door, turned on the shower. Her mum climbing the stairs, no doubt carrying a mug, as she liked to drink a hot chocolate in bed each night.

"I just realised, I really don't know anything about my sister."

The lights were dimmed inside the room and there was a siren somewhere driving past in the distance. As it got closer, the blue and red lights flashed gently through the windows and bounced off the walls, gone within seconds.

"What do you mean?"

Cam shrugged, twisted around in the bed, and thumped her pillows. "Like, I don't know her. Everything I thought I knew, is what she wanted me to know of her. All my anger at her...maybe it was all misplaced, and yet, I still don't know what to do with it."

"Are you angry with her?" Michelle asked, turning to face her. Her fingers reached up to push a strand of blonde hair out of Cam's face and back behind her ear.

"No, not really, not now."

"Camryn, what is really bothering you?" she asked, her fingers moving to gently tilt Cam's chin in her direction. This was going to be another moment where she would need to wait it out until Cam could put words to her feelings.

"I just want...I just needed..." She closed her eyes before speaking once again, more quietly this time. "I guess I am scared." She exhaled and then breathed more deeply before continuing. "I got used to a life without my family in it, and now they are back...I realise how much I want them in it."

"So, what's the problem, Sweetheart?"

"What if they leave again?"

~Yes~

Caroline was the first to wake. She felt tired and unable to relax completely in a strange bed, plus the nightmare of jetlag wasn't helping. She had given in and gotten up as the sun began to rise. It was chilly outside on the patio; the sun was yet to warm the sand. A mug of freshly brewed coffee in her hands, she looked out towards the ocean and understood in an instant why her sister had been drawn here.

Her thoughts drifted back to a time not so long ago when she would wake and look out on a similar view, only she hadn't been alone. Her on again, off again partner Andrew had been with her. The last time she saw him, they had made love and then he had kissed her goodbye as he set off on yet another mission.

"Good morning." A voice from behind her spoke gently; Michelle. Her sister-in-law stood there looking just as glamorous as she had expected her to. She didn't look like a movie star, not one that Caroline had assumed a movie star looked like anyway, but she was beautiful. Even without make-up, her skin was flawless. Caroline could understand what her little sister saw in her. Her hair swept up in a neat ponytail, she was wrapped in a towelling robe as she too cupped a mug of coffee in her hands.

"Morning." Caroline smiled. It amazed Michelle just how similar her eyes were to Camryn's, the only difference being that Caroline's looked haunted where Cam's now shone with happiness.

"Did you sleep well?"

"No, not really." She smiled again and took a sip of her drink, shutting down her memories and bringing her mind back to the present. "Jetlag has got a hold of me."

They both sat silently for a moment. Watching the waves roll in and out was rather hypnotic.

"Camryn needs you." Michelle spoke without turning to look at her.

"I know."

"So, if you can't be there for her, then it might be best if you left now," Michelle continued. This time she twisted slightly to take in the profile of her wife's sister. She was contemplative as Michelle waited for her reply.

"My intentions are to make amends with Camryn and to be there for her in any way she needs me to be." She turned herself now as she continued. "I need her too."

Michelle nodded her approval and smiled. "Help yourself to more coffee? I'm going to go back to bed for a bit longer."

Chapter Forty-One

It was a warm afternoon, but the wind was whipping up and blowing the sand around in swirls that skimmed across the ground. Cam and Caroline walked along the shore arm in arm. It was a move that Caroline had done without thinking, and she had breathed easier when Cam didn't flinched away.

"So, what did you want to talk about?" Cam asked gently. Her sister smiled shyly and stopped walking. She looked out to sea before turning back to Camryn.

"Andrew." She spoke quietly and looked back out to sea once again, her focus on something invisible in the distant.

Cam frowned. She had never heard of Andrew, and she had never seen her sister look as sad as she did this very moment. "Who is Andrew?" she probed, watching her sister intently.

"He was my lover." A single tear slid slowly down her cheek as she turned to face Camryn. "He was killed last year. A suicide bomber walked into a café in Baghdad, Andrew was inside-"

"Caroline, I'm so sorry." Cam took a step forward and pulled her sister in to her arms. The siblings stood clinging to one another still as the sun began to drop in the sky. For the first time in a long while, Caroline Thomas let herself be held by another human being.

"Do we need to go back?" Caroline asked, sniffing and wiping her face, her cheeks red from rubbing her sleeves to dry them.

"No, we just need to do whatever you need us to do," Cam responded. "Shall we sit?" Caroline nodded, and they strolled a little further along and found a spot perfect for them both to sit down next to each other. "Where did you meet Andrew?" Cam asked, reaching for her sister's hand.

Caroline smiled at the memory. "My last year at Uni. I told you I was headhunted by MI6? Well Andrew had been also, he was at a different University but we were invited to attend an open day, I guess you would call it." She laughed gently. "We were instantly drawn to one another, especially after I fell flat on my face and almost took him out too. He was very gracious and rather than laughing as some of the others had done, he offered to take me to dinner."

"Sounds like a gentleman." Cam smiled and squeezed the hand she held.

"Yes, he was. He was so handsome too. We did our training together but had to keep our relationship quiet, which was fine, neither of us wanted a relationship at the time, we were both so excited to be doing what we were doing that neither of us wanted to jeopardise it for the sake of dinner and some good sex." She chuckled at the expression on Cam's face. "Really? You're going to pull that face after I had to endure your sex-a-thon this morning?" Cam's eyes widened and her cheeks reddened, "What? you think I couldn't hear that?" Caroline grinned. "It's a good job Mother uses earplugs."

"Fair point!" Cam said, both of them bursting into laughter.

"Seriously Camryn, I was impressed. Three hours! That's a lot of stamina." Cam blushed again and playfully pushed her sister.

"What can I say, my wife is pretty."

"Yes, and she loves you. Any fool can see it."

Cam smiled as she thought of Michelle and then frowned as she realised Caroline was missing the person who had made her smile that way. "I am sorry I didn't get the chance to meet Andrew."

"Yes, he would have liked you."

"So what happened after your training?" Cam asked, wanting to know more about this side of her sister's life.

"Well, we didn't see each other for quite a while. I was sent to Oxford, but Andrew was sent straight to the Middle East. Our paths would cross randomly over the years, but never for very long. And then eight years ago I was sent to the Middle East too. I was Andrew's new boss."

"Oh."

"Yes, 'oh.' It was completely frowned upon to fraternise with colleagues, let alone your underlings, and for months we fought the temptation, we were strictly platonic, but that old attraction was always there, simmering away. One night we were in a hotel lobby waiting for a taxi when there was an explosion." She felt Camryn stiffen by her side, her hand gripping hold of her arm. "We were okay, but we lost a colleague, someone we were both friends with. I guess it drew us closer, made us realise how short life really could be. We got drunk on a very expensive bottle of brandy and then we made love."

"It's kind of romantic, like one of those old films."

"I guess it was for those few hours. In the morning he left for the office. My phone rang and that was it, I was on a plane and heading to Turkey."

"Huh, they just moved you without warning? What did Andrew say?"

"I have no idea, he was just told he had a new boss. It happened all the time, people would come and go without warning, that's just how it is," Caroline explained. It was darker now, the sun had virtually set, so they stood and began to walk back to the house

"I don't think...If Michelle was just gone the next morning, I think I'd fall apart."

"We all knew the deal, it was why we were so good at what we did, the ability to just up and leave at a moment's notice for whichever mission needed us."

"So, did you see Andrew again?"

"Yes, many times, any time we could, we would find a way. We had a secret system to tell each other where we were at any given time. If I had time off I would fly to wherever he was and vice versa. It was illicit and secretive and probably added to the excitement of seeing each other." She smiled, her eyes twinkling with mischief until a thought entered her mind and she became melancholy. "I was there...the morning he was killed. I was meeting him in that café, but my taxi was in a small accident and I was held up while the driver argued with the other driver. Otherwise I would have-"

"You would be dead too," Cam said, her eyes closed but her head tilted to the sky as she thought about that.

"Or Andrew would be alive?" Caroline asked. Cam stopped instantly and looked at her sister.

"You don't think that, do you? That you're the reason he...that it's your fault?" Caroline shook her head slowly as Cam breathed out a sigh of relief.

"No, not really, but there are moments I wonder what if."

"You can't, if there is one thing I know after Jessica, it's that it's futile to even think about the 'what ifs.' Things happen, dreadful awful things happen, and it's out of our control. Your being in that café that day would make no difference to the bomber. He would still have blown himself up, you had no control over that."

Caroline seemed to think about that as they began to walk once again. "I seem to have missed all the years where you grew up. When did you get so wise?" She nudged Cam with her arm and they both chuckled before Cam slid her arm through her sister's.

"After Jessica I had a lot of conversations with a therapist. They're not all bad." The younger blonde laughed until she noticed her sister looking serious once more. "What do you want to know?" she asked; she had seen that look so many times on the faces of friends and family.

"What happened? I know what I read in magazines and newspapers. I know the medical facts from a colleague, but what really happened? How bad was it?"

"It wasn't fun, that much I can tell you." Cam tried a smile, but it soon slipped from her face. "It was terrifying, Caroline. At first we thought Michelle had a stalker. Someone was sending her photographs with her face crossed out and we figured it was just some crazy that didn't like her new relationship with me."

"That would seem logical."

"Yeah, but it was Jessica. She had some warped idea that she could get rid of Michelle and then we would get back together and live happy ever after."

"Which obviously you didn't want?" Cam pulled a face of horror which made Caroline laugh.

"God no! You have met my wife, right? I would never give up what we have for anyone, let alone someone like Jessica. She already cheated on me, that's was how I ended up out here. I came home and found her with someone else." She turned to face Caroline again. "It was Kate."

"Kate? Your best friend, Kate?"

"Yeah, but I've since found out that it was even worse than that."

Caroline frowned. "What the hell is worse than your best friend sleeping with your girlfriend?"

Cam breathed in; she still found it hard to think about. "Jessica date raped her."

"She what?" The expression on Caroline's face was one of incredulity.

Cam nodded. "She drugged Kate, clearly she hadn't planned on my coming home when I did, but I was ill and got sent home from work." She looked away, feeling guilty again that she hadn't helped Kate. "I didn't know, ya know? I saw them together and I just assumed the worst...and then," she shook her head at the memory, "I left that day and didn't look back. Sometime later I bought a lottery ticket, won shitloads of money, and jumped on the first plane out."

"Yes, Dad mentioned the lottery ticket." She laughed before turning serious again, "He misses you."

Cam nodded at the comment. She knew at some point that she would need to address that issue. But not right now. "I'm not ready to deal with him right now."

"I gathered that much,"

"Mum explained about Celia, but it doesn't make the way he has behaved hurt any less."

"I don't think I know the full story there either," Caroline said, frowning at just how much she didn't know about her own family dynamics.

"Anyway, back to what you asked me." She filled Caroline in on the events of that day. How Jessica had been at the park. The fact that she had the kids with her and that Jessica had stabbed her in a fit of anger. How Michelle had to leave work to come and get the kids.

"You didn't call an ambulance right away? The police?" Caroline shook her head, unsure whether her sister was just brave, or stupid!

"Yeah of course, soon as I put the phone down from Paramount." Caroline was shaking her head in disbelief still. "Anyway, they got there and, you sure you want to hear all this?"

Caroline reached out and gripped Cam's biceps, staring right into her eyes, "No, I don't want to, but I need to. I need to know how my baby sister dealt with everything. I need to know you're okay now."

"I am okay," she reassured her. "My heart stopped beating in the park. They resuscitated me in the ambulance and again at the hospital. My lung had collapsed. I had a traumatic pneumothorax that put pressure on my heart. They had to operate, which is why I have the long scar that runs through my chest and the one on my back. The knife wounds are the ones that pepper my side and chest. They punctured my liver and kidneys too, but thankfully no real damage there." Cam looked around to check for passers-by; when she found none, she lifted her shirt to show her sister her flank.

"Jesus, Camryn."

"I'm okay, it took a while, but physically I am okay..." She looked away as Caroline studied her.

"But?"

Cam shrugged. "I have some issues with my scars."

"What kind of issues?"

"I'm just not comfortable with them totally, I mean, mostly I am, but sometimes I see myself and I struggle with it," she admitted. Looking away, she felt her chin being lifted.

"I think that it's okay for you to feel that way, but it's not okay for you to look away embarrassed while telling me because I won't judge you Camryn, or look at you differently."

Chapter Forty-Two

The gym was now fully open, and Kate Morris had been in charge for long enough to already make her mark. The first thing she had done was introduce the Personal Training apprentice scheme. Currently they had four local youngsters who had shown promise on their books. The café was now a smoothie bar, serving clients with protein shakes and low carb meals, and of course, coffee!

Cam wandered in and took a look around, impressed with everything she found. It had been a few weeks since she had last been in, and she was going to pay in the morning with aching limbs. Gavin hung back but kept an eye out as they walked through the free weights section and people stopped to admire the tall blonde woman that walked confidently up to the squat rack. She did some stretches while Gavin loaded up the bar. 40 kilograms would be the starting weight. She stepped in and got the bar steady across her shoulders before she bent slightly, lifted, and took it off the hook. Ten squats later, she racked it again. Gavin added some more weight and then stepped in to take his first set. They took it in turns to load and unload the bar for each other as they upped the weight on each set and put themselves through their paces.

An hour later, Cam found herself in the changing rooms, thankful that she had had the sense to build cubicle showers. She stripped off and washed the sweat away, feeling the scars with her soapy fingers as they travelled her body. When she was done, she wrapped a towel around her head and one around her body and opened the cubicle to head out to the dressing area. It was one thing stripping off in front of friends or playing along with the children, but it was another thing to do it in the open changing area of a gym. However, she hadn't noticed anyone else in the changing room when she had entered the shower, so she wasn't expecting to hear her name being called as she stepped out.

"Cam?"

She felt herself stiffen and closed her eyes as she recognised the voice. Turning slowly, she came face to bare breast with Serena. "Hey," she stuttered, subconsciously tightening her grip on the towel.

"I didn't know you worked out here too. Erin told me about it." She stood there smiling at Cam, completely naked. The tattoos, Cam noticed, covered a lot more of her than the areas she had already noticed. They intrigued Cam, if she was honest; she had always fancied getting one done, but hadn't really done much about finding anyone to do it for her.

"Uh, yeah when I get time." She noticed Serena's eyes take a downward sweep of her body before rising back up and settling on the scar that protruded from the top of the towel. "So, uh..." Cam speaking caused Serena to look up.

"I'm sorry, I didn't mean to stare. I have a...shall we say, interest in scars...they're just so...sexy." She winked and Cam blushed, "So, how'd ya get it?"

"Sorry, what?" Cam's initial embarrassment and need to hide away became more anger as she considered the question again. What kind of insensitive question was that!

"I'm sorry." She apologised again. "I just...I find it all so interesting."

"Well it's not. There's nothing interesting about any of it," she hissed, taking a step forward. "You wanna see it? What staring death in the face looks like?" Before Serena had a chance to reply, Cam dropped her towel and revealed the body she had hidden away all these months. She expected to see repulsion, for Serena to take a step backwards in horror. Instead, what she saw shocked her even more: lust. Her pupils had darkened, and she licked her lips to moisten them. Cam scooped the towel from the floor and wrapped it around herself quickly, regretting instantly what she had just done. Stepping into the cubicle, she slammed the door behind her. Wiping her face of the tears, she let her back lean against the door and then she laughed. A small chuckle erupted and turned into a guffaw that she wasn't expecting. All these weeks and months and she had been so worried about how others would perceive her new body. She knew how Michelle felt, she saw and felt the lust and love that emanated from her wife, but that was expected, wasn't it? Once she had gotten over the initial shock of it all and opened up to Michelle, it was obvious that her wife would still find her attractive...but other people? Right up until that moment with Serena, she had thought she cared whether other people found her attractive, but now she knew she didn't. It didn't matter, none of it mattered. She remembered back to Lucy at the cabin telling her she had to own it, and now she understood exactly what she meant.

~Yes~

Kate was waiting for her in the restaurant just down the street. She took a table on the veranda upstairs, overlooking the street below. Cam smiled when she spotted her. Her hair was shorter, tied up in a high ponytail. She had a tan already, and with the huge black designer shades she was rocking, she looked as much a part of LA as everyone else did. Relaxed and at ease, she turned slightly and caught sight of Cam. The smile widened as she waved and stood to greet her oldest friend.

"Hey." They kissed both cheeks and hugged briefly before taking seats opposite one another. "I saw you working out, heavy stuff."

Cam grinned. "I have to show Gavin how it's done." She winked, knowing full well that he could lift twice as much if he wanted to. She studied her friend; a light blush had appeared at the mention of Gavin's name. "Well, well, do I detect a small crush on my very handsome bodyguard?" The blush intensified.

Kate laughed and waved her off. "Oh shut up, I can't enjoy a hunk like that?"

The waitress appeared and took their drinks order. Kate picked up the menu and began to browse.

"So, you like Gav? I can put a word in." Cam chuckled.

Kate placed the menu back down on the table. "What makes you think I need your help?" She grinned before picking up the menu once more.

"Oh my god," Cam exclaimed. Kate didn't look up. Her cheeks were now glowing. "You and Gavin?"

Now Kate did return the smile.

"You sneaky pair of... how long?" She was still grinning, happy for her friend.

"We went out when you were up north," she admitted. "I forgot you said you was going away and I popped round, Gavin was there doing some paperwork and we got talking. Anyway, he asked me out and I..."

"And you?" Cam urged. The waitress reappeared and took their order. Sweet potato fries and a falafel burger for Kate; Cam went with the beef option.

"Okay, look..." Kate suddenly became serious. "I don't want to...to freak you out, okay, but..."

"Come on, spit it out."

"Alright, well I realised something when I was talking with Gavin. Ya know, he is such a decent guy, down to earth, funny, loyal..."

"Yeah, I get all that. Did ya shag?"

"Camryn, be serious!" Kate admonished with a grin. "He is a lot like you, actually."

Cam's eyes widened. "Uh huh, so you have shagged!!"

Kate laughed and tossed an olive at her. "No, we haven't, because he is a gentleman... so maybe he isn't as like you as I thought." She laughed out loudly at the look of shock that registered on Cam's face.

"Rude, just rude!" She grinned back.

Chapter Forty-Three

The drive home was a little quiet. While Kate and Cam had had lunch, Gavin had done his own thing. Two things now duelled within the confines of Cam's mind. One, was she supposed to know about the dates with Kate? She had forgotten to ask if it was a taboo subject, and she was desperate to see how much Gavin would blush when she asked about it. But, more selfishly, where did that now leave them with regards to Gavin potentially fathering their child? It wouldn't be the end of the world if they had to go down the route of finding another potential sperm donor, but it would be something else to decide and discuss later on down the path.

Traffic was heavy, and the tension in the car felt that way too. Eventually, it was Gavin who broke the silence. "I guess she told you?" he asked, eyes on the road ahead, both hands on the wheel.

Cam nodded, eyes forward. "Uh huh."

"Is that okay with you?"

She turned now to face him. His eyes were still on the road, but there was a twitch in his cheek. "Why would it be any of my business?"

He turned now, quickly, to look at her before returning his gaze back through the windscreen. "I dunno." He shrugged. "Just thought ya know, she is your friend, and maybe it's a little inappropriate for me to be interested in dating the boss's..."

"Hold up," she interrupted. "Firstly, yes, she is my friend, but so are you. And secondly, even if I am your boss and hers, what both of you do in your own time is up to you."

"Alright, good to know."

The silence returned. Gavin turned off the 110 and headed down Sunset. Once again it was Gavin who spoke. "I uh, what you asked me before...a few weeks ago?"

She felt herself stiffen. "Yeah?" She prepared herself for the gentle let-down. Her mind wandered to how she was going to tell Michelle. She wasn't sure she could deal with the amount of upset that would adorn that beautiful face.

"Okay, I'll do it."

It took a moment for his words to filter through and register. She was already coming up a plan to cheer Michelle up, maybe another trip to the lake. "You will? But what about...I mean, with Kate..."

"We've been on two dates. I like her, she's a great woman and all, but this is about me and you," he said, taking another quick glance across at her. "When we met, I was virtually living in my car. The life I have now, Cam, that's all because of you, you and your generosity and kindness to a stranger in need. What kind of man would I be if I could return that favour for a friend and I chose not to?"

There were tears welling up in her eyes; she could feel them about to burst and slide down her cheeks. He continued on and she remained silent.

"I will help you and Michelle to become parents, because I know that both of you will be the best parents to any child. And, I'll sign away any rights, on one condition."

"Okay."

"I get to be a part of their life, like an uncle, and when the time is right and he or she is old enough to understand, then we explain and leave it up to them to decide if they want me in their life as anything more than Mom's friend. And, if in the future you decide to have another, I'll do that too."

Cam nodded. "I uh..." She wiped her eyes with back of her hand. "I need to discuss all this with Michelle, but I don't see why it couldn't work."

"Just let me know what you decide. I wanna help."

~Yes~

Children ran around on the sand further down the beach. Cam stood on the deck with a bottle of beer in her hand and watched them as they ran back and forth, playing in the surf. She was reminded of the Granger children up at the lake, and she smiled as she remembered how great Michelle had been with them, the eldest one especially. She smiled to herself as she heard the telltale click-clack of heels on the floor. Michelle was home.

"I'm outside," Cam called over her shoulder towards her lover.

She felt the warm fingertips grip her shoulders and squeeze gently. "I know," the husky voice whispered against her ear.

"You took your shoes off," Cam stated with a grin.

Michelle chuckled and wrapped her arms around Cam's waist. "I wanted to surprise you."

They stood like that for a moment, both lost in thought as they watched the scene in front of them play out. Cam sighed and relaxed into her wife's embrace.

"Let's do it," she said, twisting her head to the right so she could see her wife's face. She placed the almost empty beer bottle down on the railing.

Michelle looked perplexed. "Do what? What adventure are you wanting to take me on now?"

Cam smiled. "Let's have a baby."

Michelle loosened her grip on Cam and moved around to stand in front of her. Now it was Cam's arms that moved in and around. Michelle's eyes swept over Cam's face, searching for any sign of doubt. "You're serious."

Cam nodded and smiled. "So serious, like I couldn't be any more serious! Let's have a kid...if that's what you still want?"

"Yes, absolutely, I just didn't think you were ready."

"I wasn't."

Michelle ducked down to look into Cam's eyes, smiled and leant in to kiss her, a tender, subtle kiss placed barely on her lips. "What changed your mind?"

"Everything. I saw a glimpse of how life could be, me and you with a bunch of brats running around."

Michelle playfully slapped her arm. "A bunch of brats? Just how many are you planning?"

Cam shrugged. "It doesn't matter, we can worry about the details later. I want to make babies with you."

Michelle leant in, kissed her. Their foreheads met and her arms snaked around Cam's neck. "I'm glad you changed your mind."

Cam smiled and found her mouth again, kissing her more passionately than before. She felt her hand being taken and the kiss break as Michelle smiled and led the way back into the house, walking backwards as she pulled Cam along with her.

Maria raised an eyebrow as they came inside. "Okay, I go now. Have fun and don't make me any mess!" she called after them. Grinning and shaking her head at the lovestruck couple, she pulled her cardigan around her shoulders and left the house, mumbling to herself about the things she still had to get done.

Upstairs, as clothes were discarded and kisses shared, a new bond was being formed: one of responsibility and moving forwards, of creating new life and new love.

"I can't believe we're really going to do this," Michelle whispered against Cam's lips. She melted into the kiss that followed, arms wrapping around strong shoulders.

"I can't believe I ever doubted that this is what I wanted," Cam admitted. "Seeing you with Storm and realising how great a mum you're going to be really opened my eyes."

"What else?"

"Lucy."

Michelle glared, the hot heat of jealousy hitting her cheeks instantly. Cam laughed.

"Not like that. Her scars," she explained. "Speaking with her about them. I realised that I was still letting them dictate who I am, and they're not me. They're just something I live with. I'd been hiding behind them and..." She wasn't sure if she should mention the episode with Serena at the gym, and decided it didn't matter. "What I know now is that, what happened to me? It happened and I can't change that, but that shouldn't stop us from living the life we want to."

"So, how are we going to do this?" Michelle stepped back and sat on the edge of the bed, pulling Cam with her until she straddled her lap. Her hands roamed lazily over Cam's nude back.

"Well, Gavin is onboard, he wants to help us."

Michelle squealed with delight and buried her face against Cam's chest, pulling her into a tight hold. "God, I really thought he would say no. I can't believe it." She grinned up at Cam now and Cam leant forward, kissing her firmly. Tongues tangled and danced.

"Have I told you today just how much I love you?"

Michelle smiled and shook her head. "Nope."

"Oh, how remiss of me. I love you so much it hurts, I love you so much that my heart feels like it's filled with helium and if you let me go then I'll float off to the moon and..."

"Okay, okay," Michelle laughed, "I get it, you love me!"

Cam nodded before resting her forehead against Michelle's.

"I love you too, Camryn." She rubbed her nose against Cam's. "We're going to make such an amazing family."

IF YOU ENJOYED THIS BOOK, OR ANY OF CLAIRE'S OTHER BOOKS. PLEASE TAKE A MOMENT TO LEAVE A REVIEW HTTPS://AMZN.TO/2XXZLPQ

MANY THANKS, YOUR SUPPORT IS EVERYTHING!

ABOUT THE AUTHOR

Claire lives in the UK.

She loves to travel and hang out with friends.

She supports Liverpool FC and enjoys working out her family tree, tattoos and singing along to Barbra in the car.

33998460R00166

Printed in Poland
by Amazon Fulfillment
Poland Sp. z o.o., Wrocław